Pele Mā

Pele Mā

LEGENDS OF PELE FROM KAUA'I

Frederick B. Wichman

illustrated by Christine Fayé

BAMBOO RIDGE PRESS/HONOLULU/2001

Dedicated to my grandchildren

ISBN 0-910043-63-9
Text copyright 2001 by Frederick B. Wichman
Illustrations copyright 2001 by Christine Fayé

Published by Bamboo Ridge Press

Designed by Steve Shrader

Printed in the United States

This project has been supported in part by the State Foundation on Culture and the Arts through appropriations from the Legislature of the State of Hawai'i, the Hawai'i Community Foundation, and the McInerny Foundation.

Bamboo Ridge Press is a nonprofit, tax-exempt organization formed in 1978 to foster the appreciation, understanding, and creation of literary, visual, or performing arts by, for, or about the people of Hawai'i.

This is issue #80 of *Bamboo Ridge, Journal of Hawai'i Literature and Arts*
ISSN 0733-0308

Bamboo Ridge is published twice a year. For subscription information, direct mail orders, or a catalog of our books, call or write:

Bamboo Ridge Press
P.O. Box 61781
Honolulu, Hawai'i 96839-1781
(808) 626-1481
<brinfo@bambooridge.com>
<www.bambooridge.com>

5 4 3 2 1   01 02 03 04 05

TABLE OF CONTENTS

PELE FINDS A HOME

1.

There is a pit in the east
Made red hot by Pele's fire.
How did the goddess find a home
On the slopes of Mauna Loa,
On Hawai'i nei,
Island where Wakea sleeps?

2.

Pele's canoe with red sails
Reached the island of Ni'ihau before dawn.
The sound of digging on the plain
Woke Wakea from his sleep.
Wakea asked:
Who is digging there at Halāli'i?
I, Pele, came the answer,
I am digging a pit to find fire.
A fire pit on Ni'ihau, a home for Pele?
Not so, said Wakea.
Each time you dig a hole
The sands of Halāli'i
Will cover your fire.
Ni'ihau is no place for you.
Move on!

3.

Pele's canoe with red sails
Reach Kaua'i just at dawn.
The sound of digging in the cliffs
Woke Wakea from his sleep.

Wakea asked:
Who is digging there at Kē'ē?
I, Pele, came the answer.
I am digging a pit to find fire.
A fire pit on Kaua'i, a home for Pele?
Not so, said Wakea.
Each time you dig a hole
The waters of Ka-wai-kini
Will drown your fire.
Kaua'i is no place for you.
Move on!

4.

Pele's canoe with red sails
Reached O'ahu as the sun rested on the horizon.
The sound of digging on the plain
Woke Wakea from his sleep.
Wakea asked
Who is digging there at Ālia-pa'akai?
I, Pele, came the answer,
I am digging a pit to find fire.
A fire pit on O'ahu, a home for Pele?
Not so, said Wakea.
Each time you dig a hole
The salty water of Ālia-pa'akai
Will drown your fire.
O'ahu is no place for you.
Move on!

5.

Pele's canoe with red sails
Reach Moloka'i at mid-morning.

The sound of digging on the plain
Woke Wakea from his sleep.
Wakea asked:
Who is digging there at Mauna-loa?
I, Pele, came the answer,
I am digging a pit to find fire.
A fire pit on Moloka'i, a home for Pele?
Not so, said Wakea.
Each time you dig a hole at Mauna-loa
The fearless people of Kalae
Will fill your pit with stones.
Moloka'i is no place for you.
Move on!

6.

Pele's canoe with red sails
Reached Lā-na'i at high noon.
The sound of digging on the plain
Woke Wakea from his sleep.
Wakea asked:
Who is digging there at Pālāwai?
I, Pele, came the answer,
I am digging a pit to find fire.
A fire pit on Lā-na'i, a home for Pele?
Not so, said Wakea.
Each time you dig a hole
The green pālāwai will grow
And smother your fire with pond scum.
Lā-na'i is no place for you.
Move on!

7.

Pele's canoe with red sails
Reached Ka-hoʻolawe at mid-afternoon.
The sound of digging on the plain
Woke Wakea from his sleep.
Wakea asked:
Who is digging there at Moʻa-ʻula?
I, Pele, came the answer,
I am digging a pit to find fire.
A fire pit on Ka-hoʻolawe, a home for Pele?
Not so, said Wakea.
Each time you dig a hole
Heavy gusts of the south wind
Will blow out your fire.
Ka-hoʻolawe is no place for you.
Move on!

8.

Pele's canoe with red sails
Reached Maui in the late afternoon.
The sound of digging on the plain
Woke Wakea from his sleep.
Wakea asked:
Who is digging there at Hale-a-ka-lā?
I, Pele, came the answer,
I am digging a pit to find fire.
A fire pit on Maui, a home for Pele?
Not so, said Wakea.
Each time you dig a hole
In this place that is too large,

The cold winds will chill you.
Maui is no place for you.
Move on!

9.

Pele's canoe with red sails
Reached Hawai'i as the sun floated upon the sea.
The sound of digging on the plain
Woke Wakea from his sleep.
Wakea asked:
Who is digging there at Kī-lau-ea?
I, Pele, came the answer,
I am digging a pit to find fire.
A fire pit on Hawai'i, a home for Pele?
Oh, yes, said Wakea.
Dig yourself a firepit at Kī-lau-ea,
Dig a deep pit so the fire
Will warm you there in your home.
Stop digging!
I want to sleep!

10.

There is a pit in the east
Made red hot by Pele's fire.
The goddess has found a home
On the slopes of Mauna Loa,
On Hawai'i nei,
Island where Wakea sleeps,
Warmed by Pele's fire.

Pā'ū-o-Hi'iaka

The skirt of Hiʻiaka
Pāʻū-o-Hiʻiaka

ʻOHAI AND HER SHY FRIEND that had no name lived side by side enjoying each other's company. They lived at Ka-lā-ʻihi, on the sand dunes of Mānā, where the hot sun beat down on them. Wahine-koʻolau, in her wind form, was always kind to them, blowing them gently with a breeze when the sun was very hot and from time to time bringing them little sprinkles of rain to revive them and give new life to their wilted leaves. ʻOhai was a shrub and her friend was a vine. They were small and insignificant in the life of Mānā. They had nothing to fear from anyone or anything. They spent their days watching the rich life around them.

They enjoyed the never-ending spectacle of the ocean, flat and calm one day, wild and furious with waves washing almost to their feet on another. They laughed at the antics of the many birds that lived in the swamp that lay between them and the low cliffs, and at the ocean birds, brown hunakai, the sanderling, running along the beach following each receding breaker looking for sand crabs confused by the foam; gray ʻūlili, the wandering tattler, digging out larger crabs from their holes in the sand. From time to time an ʻaukuʻu, the black crowned night heron, perched in ʻOhai's top-most branches and stared at the ocean in front and at the marsh behind. The ʻaukuʻu, they knew, was the ruling chief's spy sent to gather the news, good and bad, of all his subjects and they remained very quiet when he was there.

They also watched the Mānā people coming and going: fishermen launching their net-filled canoes and the fish they brought ashore; nimble-fingered women sitting in the shade weaving strips of makaloa reeds into mats; children playing in the breakers, flying kites, their energy so high that both ʻOhai and her friend were happy not to have legs like they did.

ʻOhai was a low-growing shrub whose branches spread out low and wide. Her leaves were covered with bristles and all the other plants, except her little friend, teased her, for their skins were smooth and shiny while hers were hairy and gray. The teasing stopped, however, when ʻOhai chose to bloom for her flowers were orange-red like the clouds at sunset or dawn and more beautiful than any other plant around her on the Mānā dunes.

ʻOhai's friend was a vine with small rounded leaves. She was very shy. Her cousin, pōhuehue, was much larger and her pink flowers outshone the smaller blue flowers of ʻOhai's friend. ʻOhai's friend was very easy to overlook and she was content to have it so. She was so small and so easily overlooked that she didn't even have a name.

Finally, 'Ohai said, "I cannot go on without calling you by your name."

"We have not had trouble with that," the little vine answered.

'Ohai shook her leaves. "I want you to have a name," she said. "Choose one."

"I cannot give myself a name," the little vine protested. Names were precious. A name said who you are, how you belonged to this world. What name would 'Ohai give her?

"Then I shall call you Inoa," 'Ohai said, "for it is a word that shows my affection for you and although we are not related, you are very dear to me."

"Thank you," the little vine said. This was a term of affection, indeed, but it was a term that 'Ohai could use on anything that she loved. The little vine drooped a little, wondering if she would ever have a real name, a name her very own. It didn't matter very much, she told herself, she was content living beside her friend.

Inoa was grateful for the shade that 'Ohai gave her, although she wished she grew on the other side of 'Ohai where the shrub's shadow would cover her in the afternoon. From their place in the dunes, they could watch everything that moved along the beach from Po'o-a-honu to Poli-hale as well as everything that moved in the great marshes. They were the first to see, not long after sunrise one day, a large canoe racing toward them.

The canoe had two hulls with a platform between them, a large mast that carried a red sail filled by the breath of Wahine-ko'olau, the wind that blew from Ni'ihau to Mānā. From the top of the mast a red pennant fluttered wildly. The giant canoe sliced green waves along its side as it skimmed along as fast as an 'iwa, a great frigate bird, soaring on the air currents. A woman with flaming red hair stood at the prow, directing the course of the canoe with firm gestures. Without slowing down, the canoe caught a wave and surfed toward the shore and hissed up onto the sand.

Far away down the beach, the two plants noticed people racing down the beach, hands waving in greetings, voices raised in a chant of welcome. Two tall kahili appeared, their bright rooster feathers gleaming in the sun, royal signs that Lima-loa, their high chief, was coming to greet the new arrivals.

"Oh!" said 'Ohai. "Who is on that canoe? Why do I feel I need to welcome her?"

"I feel that, too," Inoa said. "Let us greet her properly."

The two plants called upon their roots and their branches and their leaves. They called forth tiny buds that swelled rapidly and before the woman could jump ashore, they both burst into full bloom, 'Ohai covered with brilliant orange-red flowers, Inoa covered with small blue blossoms.

The red-haired woman jumped down from the canoe and hurried across the beach toward 'Ohai and Inoa. A little infant snuggled in her arms. The woman came directly to 'Ohai and Inoa and placed the baby in 'Ohai's shade. The baby girl looked up at the woman with wide eyes. She did not seem afraid but 'Ohai reached down a branch and tickled the baby with one of her hairy leaves. The baby giggled and waved her arms happily.

"Rest here in the shade, Hi'iaka-i-ka-poli-o-Pele, you who are clasped in my heart," the woman whispered to the baby. "There are people coming to find out who we are and there will be many speeches and much drinking of kava and it will all take a long, long time. You'll be happier here."

Then the woman turned and returned to her voyaging canoe to await the arrival of the chief of Mānā. She was right, for the ceremonies did take a long time and the speeches and chants went on and on and genealogies were recited which took even longer, for this woman was Pele, a refugee from her homeland. She had set it afire and was being pursued by her sister, already goddess of the sea, Nā-maka-o-Kaha'i. Pele was not yet a goddess and did not dare match her strength against her sister, not yet. She gave no further thought to the baby she had left in the care of 'Ohai.

The baby Hi'iaka studied 'Ohai and smiled. 'Ohai dropped a few blossoms across her brow where they tangled in the baby's luxurious black hair to form a lei po'o, a wreath around her head. Hi'iaka cooed and blew bubbles and then fell asleep. The sun climbed higher and higher into the sky. The shade cast by 'Ohai got smaller and smaller. The sun began to touch the baby's toes.

"What are we going to do?" 'Ohai asked Inoa. "Soon there will be no shade. We must move the baby!"

"How?" asked Inoa, as distressed as her friend. "We cannot move her and she is too young to crawl, even if she could see her danger."

"She will burn in the sun," 'Ohai sobbed. She tried to reach her branches further out but the relentless sun continued to move. In a short time the baby would be lying in the full sun and her tender skin would burn, both 'Ohai and Inoa realized that. There were no clouds, there seldom were, there were no trees nearby to cast a protecting shade.

"Where is that woman?" 'Ohai asked angrily. "Why has she forgotten her baby?"

Hi'iaka continued to sleep. Soon she would be in the full sun where she would remain all the long afternoon. 'Ohai tried to pull herself out of the ground by the roots but could not do it. Besides, what good would it be to kill herself? All her branches slumped. "Hi'iaka will burn," she sobbed.

"Perhaps not," Inoa replied. "Perhaps..." Perhaps, perhaps she could grow. She had always been content to be small but she had seen her cousin pōhuehue grow many feet in a single day. Perhaps ... perhaps ....

Inoa concentrated her entire being. She followed herself into the ground down into each root and rootlet, drawing strength. She pushed with all her inner strength at her growing tips, at every leaf bud, at every flower bud. She felt herself growing and growing and slowly covering the baby with a tendril, which grew and leafed and flowered, then with another tendril and yet another. Hi'iaka awoke and laughed at the tickling of the vine along her ribs. She reached baby hands to pluck at the blue flowers, for she was now covered from head to foot with leaves, which, small as they were, were enough to protect her skin from the burning sun.

Let the sun shine, Inoa thought, it cannot harm her now.

Baby and vine rested. 'Ohai remained silent and thought in wonder of her little friend.

When Pele returned, she stooped over her beloved Hi'iaka-i-ka-poli-o-Pele and reached out her hands. Then, abruptly, she pulled her hands back. She looked closely and in thought heard only by 'Ohai and Inoa, said, "I owe you my gratitude."

"No, no," protested 'Ohai, "not at all."

Inoa shyly sent out feelings of affection and Hi'iaka laughed.

"What can I do to thank you?" Pele asked.

"Nothing for me," 'Ohai said. "But you could help my friend."

"How?" asked Pele.

"She has no name," 'Ohai said. "Can you give her one?"

"That is all you ask?" Pele said in surprise.

She reached to pick up Hi'iaka from her sandy and leafy bed. Inoa cast loose her newly grown tendrils, which draped themselves around Hi'iaka's waist like a skirt of the finest tapa made of small rounded leaves and wide-petaled blue flowers.

"Your name shall be Pā'ū-o-Hi'iaka, skirt of Hi'iaka, the beloved of Pele's heart."

Thus it was that the little vine earned a name for herself. Ever after, when 'Ohai spoke to her old friend, she was always careful to call her by name, Pā'ū-o-Hi'iaka, for had they not been the first to help Pele find a home in a new land?

Ka ʻAi na Nā Manu

CHRISTINE FAYE·01

Food for Birds
Ka ʻAi na Nā Manu

PĀ-NAUNAU AND KA-UMU-PUʻE were not like most other birdcatchers, for they loved to talk and took great pleasure in always contradicting each other and arguing each and every word the other said. They were always together, their dark eyes seeing everything, for at times they could fall silent and move so carefully that no bird sitting on a nearby branch would fly away in fright. They enjoyed watching their neighbors and the strange things they did and commented on them to each other. They lived in Ka-lalau and Ka-hua-nui was their konohiki chiefess. At her command in the beginning of summer they climbed the trail out of the valley and lived for three months haunting the deep forests and venturing into the terrors of the great Alakaʻi swamp. There they caught the colorful birds, the honeycreepers, and plucked their red and yellow and green feathers. When the summer was over and the nights began to grow cold, they returned to Ka-lalau and joined the household of Ka-hua-nui and ran errands for her and did whatever else she might command of them.

They were on the beach the day an outrigger canoe with a woman with flame-colored hair sitting at the prow paddled into view. The two birdcatchers ran to tell Ka-hua-nui.

"She was exhausted," Pā-naunau said, "slumped over, weary to the very bones, her clothes tattered, the canoe wave-battered."

"She sat at the stern of her canoe," Ka-umu-puʻe said, "upright, strong, with swift strokes of her paddle sending the canoe on shore. She was strong and she seemed angry as though with each stroke of her paddle she was punishing the sea."

"Perhaps you are both right," Ka-hua-nui said, "perhaps not. Let me see for myself." Ka-hua-nui strode to the beach and waited until the canoe, with a deep stroke of paddle, caught a breaker and skimmed over the foam onto the beach. Pā-naunau and Ka-umu-puʻe pulled the canoe, still holding its rider, out of reach of the ocean.

"Greetings," Ka-hua-nui said. "Welcome. I am the konohiki of Ka-lalau."

"Greetings," replied the red-haired woman, "I am Pele and I have traveled a long time from Kahiki."

"Come and eat and rest yourself," Ka-hua-nui said.

In the days that followed, Pā-naunau and Ka-umu-puʻe gathered lauaʻe fern and brought wauke bark to Ka-hua-nui and watched her beat the two together to make a fresh, fragrant skirt for her guest. They watched as Pele regained her strength, for she had been tired. Pā-naunau was right, and yet still proud, Ka-umu-puʻe was right. The two argued and bickered happily over that and never did agree that both could be right.

Pele asked them about the birds in the mountains at the top of the curtained walls of Ka-lalau.

"They are beautiful," Pā-naunau said.

"Their feathers are brightly colored," Ka-umu-puʻe said.

"I should like to see them," Pele said.

"Take her and show her these birds," Ka-hua-nui ordered the two birdcatchers.

"It is winter time up there," Pā-naunau protested. "It will be cold, terribly cold. The birds hide in the cold."

"The birds fly when the sun shines," Ka-umu-puʻe objected.

"It will rain," Pā-naunau said.

"The sun will shine, I tell you," Ka-umu-puʻe replied.

"Enough," said Ka-hua-nui, tapping her tapa beater on her anvil impatiently. "Prepare ti leaf cloaks. Prepare your ipu holoholona, your traveling calabash, and remember to take your fire sticks with you. Yes, it will be cold," she explained to Pele, "but only at night and a fire will keep you warm."

Pele looked up to the top of the cliffs that surround the valley of Ka-lalau. It was a long way up. There were two trails, Kalou on the right hand ridge and Ālealea-lau on the left. "Which way shall we go?" Pele asked her guides.

Pā-naunau gestured to the left. "Ālealea-lau trail gets us to the top quicker."

"It is very dangerous," Ka-umu-puʻe said. "Kalou is surer; the trail is easier to follow."

They relaxed against some stones, prepared to argue contentedly over which way to go. Pele, looking at them with impatience, simply decided to walk on, following the path that seemed most used. The two birdcatchers ran to catch up to her, for Pele was tall and they were short and for each stride of the flame-haired woman they had to take two. Soon they were trotting but they were used to such exercise and had more than enough breath to continue talking.

"Ālealea-lau is quicker," Pā-naunau pointed out, but they were already far up Kalou trail between the two guarding rocks, the children of Nā'iwi.

"This is quicker," Ka-umu-puʻe said, "and besides we are already on Kalou. Where shall we take her? Ka-hua-nui did not say."

"To Pu'u-o-Kila," Pā-naunau said, "then join the road through Alaka'i swamp over to the edge of Wai-niha."

"I say we go to the meadow of Kanaloa-huluhulu, through the Menehune village of Wai-neki, and on to Ka-ua-i-ka-nanā and Ka-wai-kōī. There are many birds along the road."

"So many people go that way," Pā-naunau said. "The birds are harder to catch."

"We don't need to catch them" Ka-umu-pu'e replied. "We only need to see them."

And the two argued happily and constantly. Pele became irritated with them, their voices shrilling in her ears like the birds themselves, or the land shells singing from the mountains, a constant babble of sound. The two birdcatchers chattered on, unaware that Pele was beginning to consider them a serious nuisance. Pele was seeking a home, a place where she could dig a home for the sacred fire that lay hidden in her staff. She would have preferred silence for she was also plotting how to survive the constant onslaughts of her sister, Nā-maka-o-Kaha'i, who was following her, constantly seeking to destroy her, to cover Pele's fire with ocean and thus to destroy her.

Pele's eyes flashed. No, she would defeat Nā-maka-o-Kaha'i yet. All she needed was a home above the reach of the highest wave, then she could stoke her fires and slowly send tongues of lava flowing into Nā-maka-o-Kaha'i's ocean home and wrest new land from the sea. Pele had traveled far; she was tired, perhaps this island would give her a new home. She strode on, following the well-trodden path through the forest.

"Look!" whispered Pā-naunau, pointing to a small yellow-green bird flitting through the canopy of lehua trees, "an 'amakihi!"

"An 'anianiau," Ka-umu-pu'e corrected.

"No matter," snapped Pele. "It is a bird. I have seen it."

They continued on and reached Kanaloa-huluhulu meadow, and, after much argument between the two pot-bellied birdcatchers they crossed over a small ridge into Wai-neki, valley of wild bulrushes, until they reached the Kōke'e stream, and climbed the ridge beyond to a flat land covered with lehua and koa trees, red-berried pūkiawe shrubs and clumps of purple-berried 'uki'uki. Among them, Pele saw a shrub bearing red berries. "What is this called?" she asked.

"That is the 'ōhelo," said Ka-umu-pu'e. "The birds are very fond of it."

"Indeed," said Pā-naunau, for once in complete agreement with his friend, "it is the preferred food of the birds."

"What does it taste like?" Pele asked.

"Who knows?" Pā-naunau said. "It's bird food. I've certainly never eaten it."

"Me neither," said Ka-umu-puʻe. The birdcatchers glanced uneasily at each other. This was the second time they had actually agreed with each other.

Clouds had begun to pile up in the east and their undersides were dark. The sun was setting and the lilinoe, a fine, cold mist, began to fall. The birdcatchers set down their ipu holoholona and pulled out three ti leaf cloaks and hats.

"This will keep you dry," Ka-umu-puʻe told Pele.

"I do not need it," she replied. She did not explain that she was fire, her skin so warm that the fine mist burned away into steam before it ever touched her.

The birdcatchers however pulled on their raincoats. "It is time to stop for the night," Pā-naunau said hopefully, for Pele had not slowed down, eager to see the lay of the land before her, to find the home she so eagerly looked for.

Pele did not answer but strode through the trees until at last she stood at the edge of a ridge that led into a steep-walled valley through which a stream tumbled and sang and cascaded. On one side was a deep canyon and in front of her, stretching as far as she could see in the failing light, were hills and ridges, valleys and gulches with water pouring down them.

"What is this land?" Pele demanded.

"Alakaʻi swamp," Pā-naunau said, "where there are pools of water so deep no one can touch the bottom and where clumps of trees and bushes grow on islands that sink as you step on them."

"Waiʻaleʻale," said Ka-umu-puʻe, "where it rains every day of the year almost, where the lake ripples in the wind and feeds two mighty rivers, the Wai-niha and the Wai-lua."

"Is it a land of water?" Pele asked in dismay.

"Yes," the birdcatchers replied. "Water in the ground, water gathered in ponds, water falling as mist from the clouds, and we do not speak of the days of rain when the streams become torrents and their banks disappear."

"This is no land for me," Pele muttered. "We can return now."

"But you have not seen the birds yet," Pā-naunau protested.

"Besides it is getting dark. We must spend the night here" Ka-umu-puʻe pointed out. He led the way back for a short distance and pointed out a small tree that had elliptical leaves. It would offer some protection from the lilinoe, which was slowly changing to being a steady light rain that threatened to continue overnight.

Pele sat down. "Bring out the food," she ordered.

Pā-naunau looked expectantly at Ka-umu-puʻe. Ka-umu-puʻe said, "I thought you brought the food calabash."

"No, you were supposed to," Pā-naunau said.

"No food? Such fools," Pele said. "We will have to do without then."

For once the two birdcatchers were silent. They were now wet, cold, and hungry.

"I wish we had a fire," Pā-naunau sighed.

"Get out your fire sticks," Ka-umu-puʻe said. "Make us one."

Pā-naunau rummaged in his gourd calabash and found his fire sticks. "We need dry moss or fern and some wood," he said hopefully. The two birdcatchers stared around them in the gathering darkness. What moss they saw was wet. New fern fronds dripped water steadily on old fronds. There were no branches of dead wood lying easily to hand anywhere they could see.

"No fire," said Ka-umu-puʻe. "This will be a long night."

Pele laughed at the expressions on the birdcatchers' faces. She took pity on them and since the stars would not shine this night, she might as well look into flames of fire for comfort. "First make a small circle of stones," she ordered the two unhappy men. "Then fill it with dead wood. Never mind if it is wet." This was done and Pele thrust her staff into the middle of the woodpile. A small tendril of smoke rose, followed soon by dancing flames. The two men stretched out along the ground, their feet to the fire, too happy to be warm to care how it had come about.

"Tell me stories of these mountains," Pele said, for once welcoming the sound of their voices. Their tales kept her from remembering she was hungry.

Pā-naunau and Ka-umu-puʻe told what stories they remembered. The fire was hot and they kept shifting about from one hip to the other, supporting their weight on an elbow. Their free leg and arm swung in wide gestures, now indicating the size of giant Kanaloa-huluhulu, now imitating the slithering of Puhi, the giant eel that had come from Kahiki, as he carved out his valley, not far from where they three were now sitting. The birdcatchers kept shifting from one side to the other, for the fire was hot and their feet nearest the fire grew uncomfortable.

Pele listened to them but could not keep from wondering where she would find a home for herself. For the moment she was warm and dry but hungry. She looked about her into the forest filled with plants she had never seen before, there were many but to her eye they had a tendency to look alike. True, the greens were different, the leaf shapes were subtly different, some were tall trees, some small shrubs but still they tended to look alike. No food there.

She noticed an 'ōhelo shrub laden with red berries when a small bird flew onto a branch and began to gorge itself on the berries. If a bird could eat these berries, Pele decided, then she could herself. She rose and began to pick the berries, choosing only the most brilliant red, those that reminded her of her own beloved flames. She put one into her mouth and rolled it around on her tongue. The juice was tart but pleasant. Pele began to eat them.

"What are you doing?" Pā-naunau asked, amazed.

"Eating dinner," Pele replied.

"That is bird food," Ka-umu-pu'e replied. "Only 'amakihi eat them."

"'I'iwi eat them, too," Pā-naunau corrected.

"Not so," Ka-umu-pu'e returned. And the two old friends began to quarrel.

Pele placed a handful of berries into her mouth, then another, and another. When she had eaten enough, she returned to the fire under the tree. The two men teased her.

"If Pele chooses to eat the 'ōhelo berry," Pele said, "that is my business. Now turn your faces away and let me sleep. You may continue your arguments but I warn you do not attempt to tease me. The birds and I have full stomachs, but you do not. And you may not eat the 'ōhelo, for they are now forbidden to all but me."

With that Pele fell asleep. In the morning, the two birdcatchers brought her back to Ka-lalau and in a few days were among those that waved the red-haired stranger farewell.

In the days that followed, Pā-naunau and Ka-umu-pu'e often told of their journey to the edge of Alaka'i swamp. They demonstrated how they had lain beside the fire and Ka-hua-nui recognized that here was a possible dance and sent for students from the Hā'ena school of hula to learn the gestures. In this way the visit of Pele to Ka-lalau was remembered.

The two birdcatchers also pointed out to their friends the place where Pele had lit them a fire. The tree that had sheltered them had turned gray, smoky gray, and they called it *uahi-a-Pele*, Pele's smoke.

There were those who do not believe that Pele has the power to kapu the 'ōhelo for her own use and before continuing on their way through the swamp will pick and eat some of them. Always, always, the clouds thicken, the lilinoe falls, and soon heavy rains drench the traveler. Even today this is so, although the 'ōhelo is now very hard to find.

Kamapuaʻa, ke Mākaia

Kamapua'a, the Avenger
Kamapua'a, ke Mākaia

THE SUN SANK BELOW THE WESTERN RIDGE of Ka-weli-koa and shadows filled the valley of Kīpū-kai, until only Hā'upu peak was left in the golden afternoon sun. Farmers gathered up their tools and left their fields of yams and sweet potatoes. They did not pay attention to the 'iole, the small gray rat, or the moa, the gold- and red-feathered rooster warning them: "He miki! He miki! Be on the watch! Be alert!"

Women in their shed on the dunes overlooking the beach washed their tapa boards, beating sticks, and their brushes of hala fruit. They covered their calabashes of dyes, damped the strips of wauke still unused, and rolled up their unfinished baskets and mats. They did not pay attention to the kōlea, the golden plover, or the 'ūlili, the wandering tattler, warning them: "He miki! He miki! Be on guard, be alert!"

Children raced up and down the beach and slid down the sand dunes and jumped into the ocean for a last swim before being called home. They paid no attention to the makani kū honua, a sudden gust of wind before a storm, or the pū ki, waves breaking higher than usual as though pushed by a storm, as they warned: "He miki! He miki! Be on guard, be alert!"

The konohiki chief of Kīpū-kai, Ka-ua-koko watched with contentment for the crops were ready for the harvest in just a few days, the tapa, mats, and baskets were particularly well done, and no one was ill. The owl flew overhead, calling out, "He miki!" but Ka-ua-koko did not understand. No one heard the warning:

> "He miki! He miki!
> Na ka pua'a 'eku 'āina
> 'E kū ana i ka moku o Kaua'i!
> Ke akua maka 'iolea!
>
> Be on the watch! Be alert!
> The hog that roots up the land
> Is standing on Kaua'i!
> The god of the wild eye!"

As they came home this evening, no one felt the angry gaze that watched every move they made. No one saw the humuhumu-nukunuku-a-pua'a, the small black trigger fish with a long snout like that of a pig, as it swam in over the reef and grew larger and larger and changed shape. A huge hog, with bristles of pure black and long sharp tusks that curled from his mouth to his ear tips, climbed to its feet. The pig rooted in the sand, opening a spring of fresh water and drank its fill. Then once again this fish or hog changed its shape. Now he was tall and broad shouldered, his back covered with black bristly hair which he covered with a kihei, a cloak of undecorated tapa. Now this man, this fish, this pig, watched with angry eyes as the people of Kīpū-kai went home.

Yet what could the people of Kīpū-kai have done if they had seen all these changes? For this was Kamapua'a. Kamapua'a! A demi-god, indestructible, either a friend or a foe until death, lover of women, who could change his body, they say, into any one of four hundred different forms and so escape all his enemies. He had changed his body many times escaping from his hated uncle, Olopana of O'ahu, who was fed up with Kamapua'a's tricks and drove him from the island. It was Malae, a priest from Kaua'i, who had discovered the secret of Kamapua'a's strength and told Olopana how to defeat his nephew. Kamapua'a had sworn that Kaua'i people must pay for Malae's action. Revenge was sweet and tasty.

When the last of the Kīpū-kai residents dropped off to sleep, Kamapua'a strolled to their fields of yams and changed into the black hog with stiff bristles down his back, long sharp tusks and red glaring eyes. During that night, he tore up the fields of yams with his snout and tusks, broke down the walls with his sharp hooves and ate heartily as he went. By dawn he was tired and found an out-of-the-way place for his sleep.

The people of Kīpū-kai awoke to find their land in ruin. "Who has done this?" they asked their chief Ka-ua-koko. "It looks like a herd of pigs has worked all night, rooting and digging, but how can that be? Why did we hear nothing?"

Ka-ua-koko, who was as surprised and perplexed as any of his people, said, "We have displeased the gods somehow. Let the priests offer prayers and let us repair the damage as best we can."

Everyone worked hard, gathering what few yams and sweet potatoes had escaped destruction, smoothing out the fields to get them ready to be replanted, mending the nets, and smoothing the dents in those anvils still possible to use again. Everyone worked, even the littlest child capable of holding a cup without spilling water helped. As the sun again came to rest on the ridge of Ka-weli-koa, they grew uneasy.

"Perhaps whatever it was will come again tonight," Ka-ua-koko said, expressing the fear everyone felt. "We must stand guard."

The konohiki and his priests watched over the valley of Kīpū-kai from hidden places on the slopes of Hā'upu and Ka-weli-koa. They watched as a giant black pig tore into their sweet potato fields, digging deep with its large ivory tusks, and throwing up tubers which he gobbled. When all the fields were ruined, the first glimmering of dawn colored the eastern sky and the pig returned to his sleeping place, careless of the watchers marking where he went.

Ka-ua-koko hurriedly called together every Kīpū-kai man. "Gather all the strongest ropes we have," he ordered. "Bring the strongest fishing nets." The chief led the way to the sleeping pig. They stared fearfully at its size. They had never seen such a huge pig, like a boulder of immense size, a giant among pigs! The chief gestured and the men surrounded the sleeping hog with their nets and caught him and tied his four feet together, lashed with the strongest ropes, tied with the strongest knots.

"Return to the village!" ordered Ka-ua-koko. "Dig an oven! Gather firewood! We shall feast tonight!"

The men cut a stout branch from a tree and slid it under the ropes holding the pig's feet together. It took ten men in front and ten men in back to carry the hog to their village. The women and children circled this giant to see with their own eyes such a marvel while the men dug an oven, lit a fire, and tossed in rocks to become red hot enough to cook their captive.

By this time, the sun had crossed the sky once again and was setting below Ka-weli-koa. The pig opened his eyes slowly. He yawned and stretched. The ropes burst and the pig rolled onto his feet. The women and children ran screaming from the place. The men rushed for their spears but Kamapua'a leaped on them and tossed them into the air with his tusks and trampled them under his sharp hooves. He considered killing them all but instead he roamed between the houses, broke holes in their thatched walls, broke the gourd calabashes holding clothing, and tore the woven mats under his razor sharp hooves. He wandered to the shore, laughing at the way people ran from him, fearful for their lives. He tore apart the fishermen's nets. He laid waste to the sheds where tapa was beaten and mats were woven.

Then he climbed the trail leading to the pass between Kīpū-kai and Kīpū-uka and came to the spring whose sweet waters fed all the fields of Kīpū-kai. He stepped into the pond and let the water cover him and wash him clean. After his bath, he smiled in contentment. The spring would always now smell of pig and its water would never again bring life to plants but only death. He had avenged the insult of Malae. Little did he dream that red-haired Pele, whom he would soon meet on the plains of Hā'iku, would laugh until tears poured down her cheeks, looking at the pitiful damage he had done.

Clean and contented he fell asleep beside the trail, resembling one of the large black rocks that dotted the slopes around him.

The people of Kīpū-kai however dared not sleep that night. In the morning they saw in despair the damage the giant pig had brought to them. "Who has done this?" they asked. The kilokilo, priest, whose duty it was to ask the gods for answers to questions such as this, stared into his calabash and watched the images the gods sent him. The answer did not please him for who can fight against a demi-god and win? But at least, the kilokilo could warn others to be on their guard:

"Be on the watch! Be alert!
The hog that roots up the land
Is standing on Kaua'i!
The god of the wild eye!"

He Kaʻao a Lima-loa

CHRISTINE FAYE · 01

A Story of Lima-loa
He Ka'ao a Lima-loa

LIMA-LOA ROSE TO HIS FEET and stretched his cramped muscles. He had slept sitting against a large boulder whose stored heat had kept him warm through the night. He looked down from his perch in the pass between Kīpū-uka and Kīpū-kai, down over the rolling plains of Ha'ikū where the armies of Puna and Kona faced each other. There was no sign of movement. No dust clouds eddied in this morning's storm-driven wind. No white flags fluttered to tell of priests praying to their feathered gods for victory this day. The armies were still asleep, he thought, because no battles were planned for this day, which already promised storm-driven rain. There was no need for him to rush to the battlefield where day after blood-soaked day the two armies fought with neither side gaining a lasting advantage.

He could spend the day trying to win the hearts of the two maidens who guarded Ke-mamo spring. Their names were Kukui-lau-mānienie and Kukui-lau-hanahana. They were closely related to Kūkona, the ruling chief of Puna. Each was as lovely as the full moon, with skins that reflected the silvery sheen of the kukui trees for which they were named. Yet like every other woman he had ever sought, they refused to clasp him in their arms. Why did he always have such trouble with women?

Lima-loa was a giant of a man, with the body of a trained athlete and warrior. He had looked at himself in a quiet pond once and decided that he did not look too different from all the other warriors he knew. Yet they were able to attract women and somehow he couldn't. Women teased him, turned their backs on him, refused him, and he did not know why. As a boy, he played with his brother Lohia'u and his sister Ka-hua-nui in Ka-lalau valley and at Hā'ena at the hula school. His problems began when he became a young man. Girls fell into Lohia'u's arms, eager for his embrace. The same girls laughed at Lima-loa. Kilioe, chiefess of the hula school, took him aside one day and, placing her hands on his head, stared into the distance for some time. Then she shook her head sorrowfully. "I am sorry," she said, "for you have already been chosen and marked. She has placed her taboo over you. You must wait until the lady of the twilight calls you to her. But somehow I do not think you will find her at twilight. I can tell you nothing more."

Still he would never give up. Somewhere the woman of the twilight was waiting for him and someday he would find her. Perhaps either Kukui-lau-mānienie or Kukui-lau-hanahana was that woman. He lived on hope. Yet he had nothing more to offer these maidens of Ke-mamo. He'd already given them all he had brought with him and they had laughed and refused to listen to his pleas to become his lover, one or the other or both. Maybe if he could separate them? It would be easier to whisper soft words into one set of ears. He needed to find something to give them as a present, some gift they would really appreciate.

Just then he heard a confused murmur of excited shouts and wailing cries behind him and turned to look down into the valley of Kīpū-kai. He saw people running here and there like a flock of disturbed chickens. He noted that they must have harvested their fields of yams and sweet potatoes and that seemed strange because normally farmers planted only a little at a time and never completely cleared their fields as they were now. Curious, he started down the trail.

As he came around a zigzag bend, he saw a huge pig lying below him alongside the trail. It would make excellent eating and if he could take it back to the lovely women that guarded Ke-mamo spring, perhaps they would pay attention to him and learn to love him. His left hand clenched, seeking his spear. He grunted, for he was unarmed. He had given his weapons to the Kukui sisters but, as usual, they had only teased him and laughed at him, and sent him away to sleep with his back against a stone rather than in their arms.

Lima-loa found a large boulder in a direct line above the hog and leaned into it. The boulder budged and began to roll down the hill toward the sleeping pig.

Lima-loa gaped wide-eyed as the pig suddenly woke and stood. What he had thought was a pig was a man almost as large as Lima-loa himself, his body covered with coarse black hair. The man tossed a handful of rocks under the boulder that was almost on top of him. Two small rocks wedged tightly under the boulder, bringing it to a stop.

The man looked up at Lima-loa. Lima-loa still thought he looked like a pig, a big flaring nose that had been broken many times, thick lips, an unusually hairy body. It was obvious that he was a trained warrior, too. Muscles such as those were never found on commoners.

"Good morning," the stranger called as he started up the path. His bright shining eyes studied the man who had just tried to kill him. Already he was plotting revenge on this powerful warrior who had dared to attack him. "My name is Kamapua'a."

"I am called Lima-loa," he stammered. "When I first saw you I thought you were a pig. I hope you are not hurt."

"I am not hurt," Kamapua'a said, and wondered how to get his revenge.

The two men studied each other, deciding whether to issue a challenge on the spot or to become friends. Kamapua'a saw the story of Lima-loa's life in the freshly healed wounds on his body, wounds only a strong, cunning warrior would receive. He saw that Lima-loa was a simple man and he would be a good friend to have behind one's back on a battlefield. Lima-loa knew that friends were not easy to come by and perhaps this man knew tricks that could help him on the battlefield of men and the harder problems of wooing women.

Both men offered the other their hands in friendship.

Kampua'a said, "You look as though you have been wounded."

"Not in battle," Lima-loa said. "By two women."

Kamapua'a grinned. He had never had trouble with women. "They have rejected you? Don't give up."

"Maybe you can help me," Lima-loa said. "The two are always together and one can't woo one alone. If you were to talk with one while I talk to the other, maybe we will both be lucky."

"And what if I win them both?" asked Kamapua'a. "What then?"

"Why, we will be friends," Lima-loa answered. "It does not seem to be my fate to have a wife and I would rather have our friendship even if they both reject me and take you."

Kamapua'a laughed to himself. No man could willingly give up a lover to another without pangs of hot jealousy. Perhaps he and Lima-loa would fight one another yet. He liked the idea of winning the two women and leaving Lima-loa neither. For if the two fought, Lima-loa would be careless in his rage. Revenge is sweet, Kamapua'a thought.

"Where are these women?" Kamapua'a asked.

Lima-loa led the way back up the trail. When they reached the top, Lima-loa said, "You can see them from here as they bathe in their pond."

The two men hid behind a large boulder and peered down. Kukui-lau-mānienie and Kukui-lau-hanahana were washing their hair, crushing buds of ginger and rubbing its rich lather into their hair before rinsing it in the pond outlet. They knew they were greatly desired by any man who saw them but they cared for none and drove them away. The sisters were always together. It was never possible for a man to find one of them alone and he could not woo one without the other being present and laughing at him. They chattered to each other about Lima-loa who had tried to win them both. Little by little he gave them all he possessed, his feather cape, his helmet, his spear, his war club, his sleeping mats, his feather lei, everything he owned he laid at their feet.

"Nothing you give us will make us change our minds," Kukui-lau-hanahana had warned.

"Go away!" Kukui-lau-mānienie had ordered.

They had laughed and splashed water at Lima-loa. They had looked into the sacred waters of Ke-mamo and there they had admired their own reflections and had never seen the shadow of the man they would love. They had allowed Lima-loa to kneel and drink from the spring but he had not cast a reflection and they knew he was not for them.

They were so used to being stared at that they did not feel the hot, lustful eyes of the two warriors who spied on them as they bathed in the clear waters of Ke-mamo spring. As soon as he had taken in all their beauty, Kamapua'a knew they must become his.

Kamapua'a whispered, "Are these your girls, Lima-loa?"

"Yes," replied the giant.

Kamapua'a nodded happily. "They are very beautiful," he said. "Let me see what I can do. You wait here until I call you."

Kamapua'a walked down a little ways, chanting a song of greetings to the two maidens.

> "I am like a man when in love,
> When overcome with love,
> Made ill at ease by the women of Ke-mamo,
> Kukui-lau-mānienie and Kukui-lau-hanahana,
> The red blossom and the white blossom.
> What are the two of you doing here?
> Are you spending your time in the uplands,
> Mating with a lover?
> My greetings to you!"

The two young women stared into the pond and saw the reflection of the stranger's face in the still waters. The magic of the Ke-mamo cast its spell and Kukui-lau-mānienie and Kukui-lau-hanahana fell in love. They did not know they were in the presence of a demi-god, part man, part hog, nor did they care.

"How can we dally with a lover?" laughed Kukui-lau-mānienie, answering the stranger's chant.

"When there is no one lover for us both?" giggled Kukui-lau-hanahana.

Kamapua'a grinned. "Here I am," he said.

The women sighed. "Come home with us, then," Kukui-lau-mānienie invited.

"Willingly," Kamapua'a said. As he followed them into their sleeping house, he glanced up the trail where Lima-loa was waiting. Kamapua'a chuckled. He would have a long wait. He had so easily trapped the two and Lima-loa had neither. Revenge, thought Kamapua'a, was sweet. He walked away, strutting between the giggling sisters.

Revenge, however, needs its victim to feel the great pain vengeance demands. Kamapua'a did not see Lima-loa's smile. Since they were not destined to be his, he thought, let them belong to his new friend.

He remembered his dream, one he had so often come to him over the years, all those years when he had trained himself in war skills, boxing, wrestling, spear handling, dagger strokes. He never missed when he spun a water polished stone from his sling. He learned as many strokes of the war club as he could find men who knew them. He continued to grow in height, girth, and war-like knowledge. He traveled down the chain of islands to Hawai'i, seeking new masters to teach him and looking for the mysterious woman of the twilight, the woman he sought.

In this dream, he was in his house and putting on his feather cloak and feather helmet and had placed his lei 'opu'u around his neck. He grabbed his spear and left the house. All around him were other houses shaded by coconut trees. A path of crushed coral led to a house larger than any other in the village, and Lima-loa walked down the path eagerly for he knew the lady of the twilight awaited him impatiently.

Someday he would find her. Lima-loa smiled and sighed and looked out over the battlefield. Unlucky in love, he would be lucky in war. Let Kamapua'a have the pleasure of revenge. He had his dream of a lovely woman waiting just for him.

Kamapua'a, ke Koa Po'ohuna

KAMAPUA‘A, THE HIDDEN WARRIOR
Kamapua‘a, ke Koa Po‘ohuna

KUKUI-LAU-MĀNIENIE AND HER SISTER KUKUI-LAU-HANAHANA were miserable. Once they had been carefree, caring for no one but themselves, free to tease all the young men who came to Ke-mamo, the spring on the slopes of Hā‘upu mountain, to visit with them in high hopes. Once they had been beautiful. Now they had so much to do they scarcely had time to comb their hair. Ever since they had seen Kamapua‘a's reflection in their spring and fallen in love themselves, ever since they had married the man with pig-like manners, their beauty had begun to fade, the young men had stopped coming, and their fingers became red and rough with the work they were forced to do.

The sisters prepared all the food that their husband Kamapua‘a gobbled down. Every anahulu, every ten days, they pounded out a long strip of tapa and stamped intricate designs onto it, all so he could wrap it around his waist before strutting off to visit with his friends. They wove hala leaves into fine mats and carried them to the far away sea to wash and dry them in the sun, to make his bed thicker, deeper and more comfortable. They were lucky if they had time to gather fern to make a bed for themselves before sundown. From morning to night they worked hard for they had learned to be afraid of his anger.

All too often, as now, Kamapua‘a came to the doorway of the sleeping house to shout angrily, "Wives! Where are you?"

"Here!" they called and ran to see what their husband wanted.

"Lazy, good-for-nothings!" Kamapua‘a snarled. "Why is my floor mat so dirty? Go and clean it."

The wives of Kamapua‘a looked at the mats and wondered. The mat was as dirty and torn as only a pig could foul it. But how had a pig entered the house where Kamapua‘a was sleeping? Kamapua‘a was glaring at them angrily. Kukui-lau-mānienie and Kukui-lau-hanahana sighed, rolled up the mat, slung it between them, and went down to the sea to clean and mend it.

When they returned there would still be the work they should have been doing, several hours worth. They would miss all the excitement that came with watching the battles on the plains of Hā‘ikū. The kingdom of Kona, led by Makali‘i, and the kingdom of Puna, led by Kūkona, were at war. Fierce hand battles were fought daily but both sides were strong and neither could defeat the other. Each battle ended with both armies separating for the night to prepare for another battle the next day. From their place beside Ke-mamo spring, far up the slopes of Hāʻupu mountain, the sisters could watch and cheer on their cousin Kūkona.

Once they had watched in dismay as the Puna army was pushed back to the Kilohana hill-top. They could see Kūkona himself, wearing a helmet and cloak of brilliant yellow and red feathers. Only the coming darkness of night had saved Puna then. Alarmed and frightened the sisters rushed to the sleeping house, calling their husband as they ran.

"Kamapuaʻa! Wake up! Do something!"

Kamapuaʻa yawned. "Do what? I'll eat. Where's the food?"

"How strangely you behave!" Kukui-lau-mānienie said. "Here you are, doing nothing but sleeping in the house."

"Our chief Kūkona was almost killed today. If he had been, you would have known nothing about it at all!" sputtered Kukui-lau-hanahana.

"The battle came nowhere near you," Kamapuaʻa replied. "Besides I do not think Kūkona will lose the war. I hear there is a strong warrior fighting with him"

"How would you know?" Kukui-lau-mānienie retorted.

"You're never awake," Kukui-lau-hanahana said bitterly.

Kamapuaʻa stood suddenly. "Get my food," he snarled, "and cease talking. I need peace and quiet." The startled sisters swore later that they saw the small bloodshot eyes, long snout and curved tusks of an enraged boar and, terrified, rushed to feed him.

He returned to his bed while they continued their countless chores.

As the sisters trudged down to the sea that day with the soiled mat drooping between them, they decided that they had had enough. Their anger grew with each step they took.

"We must punish him," Kukui-lau-mānienie muttered.

"We were happier when we had no husband," agreed Kukui-lau-hanahana.

"There was always somebody around we could tease," sighed Kukui-lau-mānienie.

They reminisced about former suitors and passed several hours without thinking of their husband. They never guessed that the pig who fouled their mat was their own husband, Kamapuaʻa.

Kampuaʻa himself dirtied the mat in his sleeping house so he could send his wives to the sea to clean it, a chore that took several hours' time. He did not want them to know that he went down to the battlefield in their absence. He, too, had watched the battles with glittering eyes. The ruling chief of Kona was Makaliʻi and Kamapuaʻa hated him, for they had often fought each other when they lived on Oʻahu. Only Kamapuaʻa's promise to his grandmother not to kill Makaliʻi had saved his life. Kamapuaʻa laughed to himself. Makaliʻi would not expect to see Kamapuaʻa on this battlefield. So, thought Kamapuaʻa, he will not see me.

Kamapuaʻa prayed to his gods and his body began to fade away until only his left hand remained visible. With this hand he grabbed up his mighty war club and ran down to join the fight. In the confusion of battling men and the dust their feet stirred up, at first no one noticed that there was a war club in their midst with no warrior wielding it. Kamapuaʻa had no trouble coming up to a Kona chief and clubbing him down. At first no one paid attention that this single hand then stripped the fallen chief of his helmet and cape which then disappeared from sight.

Day after day Kona chiefs died and Kamapuaʻa's bed grew higher and higher because of the capes and helmets hidden there. Kona warriors became terrified of the massive war club held in the hand of some invisible being. Kona soldiers watched as their companions were knocked down, dead or dying, whenever it appeared on the battlefield. How could they defend themselves against this apparition that appeared among them like the wind whose presence can be felt but never seen?

They convinced themselves that some evil Puna priest was working to destroy them. The priests they consulted could not tell them what was happening, by whom, or why. "I have prayed to the gods and offered many sacrifices," their kahuna told them. "They tell me that this is a man, although not quite like any other. He has a power different from any I have ever known before. But it is a man, not a supernatural being." Somehow that did little to cure their fear.

During one intense bout of fighting, a spear thrown from a distance struck the visible thumb. Blood flowed freely down to the wrist and dripped onto the ground. Whatever it was, this thing could bleed as well as any of them. The Kona men were a bit braver that day.

That evening Kūkona asked to have all the helmets and capes that had been taken from the dead chiefs brought for him to inspect. Whenever a chief fell on the battlefield, these insignias of his rank became the property of the ruling chief and were automatically collected from the battlefield for him.

Lima-loa, the giant warrior from Hāʻena who was Kūkona's ilāmuku, his marshal, said, "No helmets or capes were collected in the last ten days."

Kūkona angrily demanded, "Who is in charge of collecting these things?"

"I am," replied Lima-loa. "As always, when the day's fighting is done, I go among the dead to collect their insignia. I found their bodies, but they were stripped. I have asked our soldiers, but no one reports seeing anyone taking them. Only the hand makes them disappear, they say."

The soldiers of Puna had been well aware of the mysterious hand as it destroyed their enemies. After a few fearful days they knew the hand and war club did not strike them. Whoever or whatever it was, it was a friend. Then why, Kūkona wondered, was it taking the feathered plunder that belonged to him?

Kūkona turned to his kahuna, Hulu-'iwi. "What is to be done?" he demanded.

"O Haku," Hulu-'iwi said, "we must build a small platform, large enough for you, your ilā-muku and me to stand on. Then we must summon all your army. When all are gathered, you will order everyone to raise their left hand, for we know that the mysterious hand was wounded today. We need only look for the wound to know the thief."

"It is one of our men?" Kūkona asked suspiciously.

"Perhaps," replied the kahuna, "but in this way we will know who it is."

"So be it," said Kūkona. "Let the platform be built."

Early the next morning, Kūkona stood on the platform with Lima-loa and Hulu-'iwi on either side of him. Before them stood the entire Puna army.

"Raise your hands!" Kūkona ordered. Thousands of hands shot into the air and remained there until one by one the three inspected them.

"There is no wounded thumb here," said Lima-loa.

"You said we would know who it is," Kūkona said to Hulu-'iwi angrily. "That was a lie!"

"Not so," replied the kahuna calmly. "Tell me, are all your men here?"

"Of course they are!" snarled Kūkona.

"Where is the husband of your cousins?" Hulu-'iwi asked. "I do not see Kamapua'a here."

It was true. Kamapua'a was not there. "We will go find him," Kūkona said and led the way to the spring of Ke-mamo.

Kamapua'a met them at the entrance to his house, stretching his arms wide and yawning for he had just gotten up from his night's sleep.

"Look!" exclaimed Lima-loa. "His thumb!" There was a scarcely closed wound on Kamapua'a's thumb.

"Search his house!" Kūkona ordered. Lima-loa entered the house and in a few moments ducked through the doorway, his arms filled with feathered capes.

Kūkona was enraged. "Why did you take what is mine?" he demanded.

"I was guarding them until you came for me," Kamapuaʻa replied. "After all, I captured them on the battlefield. No one else." Kamapuaʻa smiled and the soldiers nearest him stepped backwards away from the fierceness of his teeth. "Take them. They are yours," he said.

"When I did not see you on the battlefield, "Kūkona said, "I took you for a coward. Now I see that is not so. I see you now and I am listening. What do you want of me?"

"Instead of a high chief speaking only to a warrior, "Kamapuaʻa replied, "we now speak man to man. Tomorrow let you, me, and Lima-loa there go onto the battlefield together. We shall challenge their best remaining warriors to single combat. By nightfall, Kona will be yours. I only ask that I be the one to challenge Makaliʻi."

"So be it," Kūkona replied and gestured to his attendants to gather up the cloaks and helmets and without a word more returned to his camp.

The sisters were furious. They realized why they had been sent away to clean dirty mats so often and how little Kamapuaʻa trusted them. They began scolding him. He held up his hand and glared at them through bloodshot eyes so fiercely they abruptly fell silent and scurried away.

Kukui-lau-hanahana whispered angrily, "Let's hide the spring!"

"He shall not drink the water or bathe in the pool again," agreed Kukui-lau-mānienie.

They covered Ke-mamo with such skill that no one could tell a spring of water was there, feeding a deep bathing pool. Then they hid themselves and waited.

When his wives did not return with his food and drink, Kamapuaʻa strode down the path to Ke-mamo. He called to his wives, "Bring me some water!"

They would not answer him. They watched with merry eyes as he searched for the spring they had so cleverly hidden. They giggled as he dug here and there with his spear, grunting and snarling. The sisters began laughing.

"Look at him," Kukui-lau-mānienie sneered, "rooting like a pig!"

"All nose, and tusk, all to no purpose!" taunted Kukui-lau-hanahana.

"Bring me water to drink," Kamapuaʻa demanded.

"Find it!" the sisters replied.

He stood still. He smelled water and he smelled the spell the sisters had thrown over Ke-mamo. He broke the spell and the spring once more was visible and so were the sisters, their faces contorted with angry mocking laughter.

Kamapuaʻa rushed at them. He grabbed Kukui-lau-mānienie and threw her into the air. Her body changed into a large rock and fell on one side of Ke-mamo spring. Then he caught Kukui-lau-hanahana and threw her into the air and she changed into a rock as she fell on the other side of the spring.

Kamapuaʻa drank his fill and bathed in the spring. He returned to his bed and slept peacefully. Before dawn he walked down the path to find Kūkona and Lima-loa waiting for him. He never looked back at Kukui-lau-hanahana and Kukui-lau-mānienie.

Ke Kaua Panina

THE LAST BATTLE
Ke Kaua Panina

KAMAPUA'A BARELY LISTENED TO THE HAKU MELE, a chanter who enjoyed the sound of his own voice as he told long tales of a long war. Kūkona, ruling chief of Puna, sat on one side of him and Lima-loa, warrior of Hā'ena, sat on the other. Both listened carefully, ignoring the food spread out before them.

The war between Kona, the kingdom that stretched from Milo-li'i to Mā-hā'ule-pū, and Puna, the kingdom that lay between the Maka-leha and Hā'upu mountains, had gone on for three generations. It began, the haku mele chanted, when Ka-'ili-lau-o-ke-koa, lovely granddaughter of Mo'ikeha and heir to the Puna kingdom had refused to marry Keli'iloa, prince of Kona. When Keli'iloa tried to kill Ka-'ili-lau-o-ke-koa's husband, the first battle was fought.

Since then there had been many battles and many heros. Palila of Puna had defeated Nā-maka-o-ka-lani of Kona before he left Kaua'i to become the ruling chief of Hilo. Ka-u'i-lani had defeated Akua-pehu-'ale of Kona and regained his father's kingdom. The battles still raged.

Kamapua'a sat between Kūkona and Lima-loa. He continued stuffing raw fish into his mouth with his right hand followed by fingers of poi with his left hand. He sucked, slurped, snorted and reminded the haku mele of the way pigs eat. However, since he was Kūkona's guest, he ignored him. To cover the noise of Kamapua'a's eating, the haku mele spoke louder and so Kamapua'a had no trouble hearing what he was saying. A lot of noise about very little, he thought.

When the haku mele had finally finished, Kūkona sighed. "If only we could win, once and for all, then this warfare would stop."

"Who is the ruler of Kona?" asked Kamapua'a, spraying stray bits of food from his too-full mouth.

"Makali'i," replied Lima-loa. "He was on O'ahu but I hear he got into trouble of some sort there and came home. Fortunately for him his father died and he inherited the kingdom."

Kamapua'a laughed. "I know Makali'i," he explained. "He will be as easy to defeat as a high wind easily knocks down a banana stalk."

"Boastful words," said Kūkona.

Kamapua'a's face darkened.

"No, no," Kūkona said quickly, "Not yours. I was thinking what Makali'i said, that Puna is a ripe fruit, close to rotten and hardly worth the picking."

Kamapuaʻa relaxed. "I think he has named the wrong kingdom," he said. "What say we go out on the battlefield and get this whole thing over with?" With that, he stood up and gestured to Lima-loa and Kūkona. "Come with me," he ordered. "We don't need anybody else."

Kūkona picked up his war club. It once had belonged to Ka-uʻi-lani, and was carved from kauila wood. A row of jagged shark's teeth had been imbedded in the highly oiled wood. It was huge, no common man could wield it. Kūkona had no trouble swinging it over his head, twirling it up one side of his body to the other. It was a formidable weapon in the hands of a formidable warrior.

Lima-loa also swirled his war club in a series of threatening gestures, designed to strike terror in the hearts of his opponents. The club was larger than that of Kūkona, bigger all around, and, instead of shark's teeth, it had an enlarged head full of sharp pointed lumps. Lima-loa himself was huge, a giant living up to his name "Long arm" and as the war club blurred in the speed with which he wielded it, he was indeed a sight to inspire fear.

Kamapuaʻa bore a striking resemblance to a black boar. His skin was covered with black, wiry hair, his arms, his chest, his back, his legs. When he grimaced, showing his teeth, terror-struck warriors swore they had seen tusks gleaming along his bearded chin. Nonetheless, beneath all that hair, muscles rippled, strong muscles capable of winning any battle, from war club to hand-to-hand wrestling. He was not a sweet piglet, a pet in a woman's arms. He was like a boar, smart, cunning, ferocious and highly dangerous.

Kamapuaʻa picked up his war club Ka-hiki-kolo and slung it over his shoulder. It was made from a branch of a koa tree that sprawled along the ground because it, alone of its kind, had no trunk. The club was very heavy but Kamapuaʻa did not seem to notice that.

"Let's go," Kamapuaʻa said. Kūkona and Lima-loa followed him across the Puna plains until they came to Ka-hoa-ea hill, where the ridge from Hāʻupu mountain reaches the plains of Haʻikū. They looked down on the plains between them and Ka-moʻo-loa ridge where the army of Makaliʻi guarded the entrance to Kona.

Kamapuaʻa cupped his mouth and yelled, "Who will fight me one on one? Who of you chicken-livered cowards dare to fight Kamapuaʻa?"

Immediately the insult brought a man out of the crowd. He was Ahu-lī, a warrior from Maka-weli. He came dancing up toward Kamapuaʻa who was trudging down towards him. As Ahu-lī neared, he called out, "I do not see a warrior." He looked about with mock surprise. "All I see is a pig, a big hairy pig."

"Hit him if you dare," said Kamapua'a, placing the end of his club on the ground in front of him. His eyes became tinged with angry red. "Yours is the first hit, mine the last."

Ahu-lī laughed, swung his war club and using the stroke called Ka-hau-komo, the coming blow, struck at Kamapua'a. Kamapua'a barely shifted his own club in the movement called Hiki-kolo and sent the club flying from Ahu-lī's hands. Ahu-lī watched, mouth agape, as his club flew through the air. Then, realizing he was now weaponless, he turned and ran. Kamapua'a with one hand merely flicked his club. It landed with a solid blow, with a sound of a melon splitting open, and Ahu-lī fell dead.

Kamapua'a turned to his companions. "This is too easy. The war will be over before nightfall."

"The war is not over yet," Lima-loa said, pointing to another Kona warrior coming toward him. "Let me have him."

"Not yet," said Kamapua'a. "I've barely warmed up." He advanced toward the newcomer, Ka-nākea.

Ka-nākea made a ferocious face and stuck out his tongue insultingly. "Your time has come," he said, "oh, black pig, just right for our sacrifice to the gods tonight."

"Yours is the first hit, mine the last," Kamapua'a said. His eyes grew darker red.

Ka-nākea raised his club and swung at Kamapua'a with the stroke Mālama-kūloko, watch within. Kamapua'a deflected the blow with Mālama-kūwaho, watch without. Ka-nākea recovered instantly and tried another stroke, Alapi'i-a-ka-'ōpae, stairway of the shrimp, one designed to strike an opponent in the chest, breaking ribs. Kamapua'a sidestepped it and sent Ka-nākea's war club tumbling end over end. Ka-nākea took to his heels and hid himself under a medium-sized tree, the red-berried 'a'ali'i. Sweeping his club in a low swing just off the ground, Kamapua'a uprooted the tree and sent the warrior's limp body flying.

Two Kona warriors rushed toward Kamapua'a, 'Ōmaumau-kīoe from the right and 'Owalawala-he'e-kio from the left. They were twins and mirror images of each other, for 'Ōmau-mau-kīoe was left-handed and 'Owalawala-he'e-kio was right-handed. They always fought togeth-er since they had learned that few warriors were adept with both right and left hands and one or the other of the twins could always overpower him. The twins were also skillful in throwing the spear. They came running up, brandishing their spears.

Kamapua'a laughed. He flipped the end of his malo in a gesture of contempt. "Throw your spears at me!" he dared them. They threw their spears, left-handed and right-handed, but Kamapua'a twisted and turned and dodged and the spears missed their mark and instead caught a rat hiding under a clump of grass. It squeaked and Kamapua'a turned to look but in an instant he turned back to the twin warriors.

But 'Owalawala-he'e-kio and 'Ōmaumau-kīoe had not wasted that instant. As soon as they saw their spears had missed the mark, they turned and ran and before Kamapua'a could get at them, they were out of sight.

"Well done," Kūkona said, still laughing. "They must be descendants of the famous runners of long ago who could bring a fish still alive from Ka-lalau to Wai-lua."

Just then another warrior approached, Kamapua'a recognized him as his own brother, Kahiki-honua-kele. What to do? He did not want his brother dead, certainly not at his own hands. Kamapua'a pointed to Kahiki-honua-kele and said to Lima-loa, "This one is yours."

With a roar of delight Lima-loa ran toward Kahiki-honua-kele. After a few insults, both men raised their clubs. Lima-loa used the stroke Ka-limu-kā-kanaka-o-Mahamoku, man-striking moss of Mahamoku. Kahiki-honua-kele fell to the ground, blood pouring from his scalp. Lima-loa raised his club to make a final ending of the Kona warrior, but Kamapua'a caught the end of the club before it could fall. "I'll finish this," he told Lima-loa. "You go down and see how many more warriors you can kill. This war must be over before nightfall."

Lima-loa saw the enemy forces gathering and grinned. He started toward another warrior, an older man than this one, but Kamapua'a said, "No, leave this one for Kūkona," and Lima-loa ran down and soon was engaged in hand-to-hand combat.

Kamapua'a had recognized the older warrior as his father, Kahiki-'ula. He turned his back on him so that he would not be recognized. "This one is yours," he said to Kūkona. Kūkona met the Kona foe and traded insults and blows but within minutes, Kahiki-'ula was stretched out on the ground, bleeding from the blow to his skull. Kūkona pulled his dagger to finish the life of the Kona warrior but Kamapua'a caught his hand. "Go down and join Lima-loa," he said. "I'll finish this and join you."

Kūkona ran to join Lima-loa. Dust flew up from all the scuffling feet and no one saw Kamapua'a as he pulled the bodies of his brother and his father toward a little stream, and sprinkled water over them. When they woke groggily, Kamapua'a told them, "You are lucky to be alive. Go now and return to your homes in Ka-lalau valley. Go, or I will kill you myself." This last he said so ferociously that the two men rose and ran. When they were out of sight, Kamapua'a went down to the battlefield and soon was shoulder to shoulder with Lima-loa and Kūkona.

The Kona warriors suddenly stood back, stilled their weapons, and looked toward a tall, broad-shouldered chief, wearing a feathered helmet and armed with a formidable club.

"That is Makali'i himself," said Kūkona. "It is my place to fight him."

"No," said Kamapua'a. "I claim the right to fight him first. I have fought him before and I am not afraid of him. Besides, after a few words from me, he will simply run away."

Lima-loa said, "Makali'i is a brave soldier and he will not run away."

"Oh, yes, he will," laughed Kamapua'a. "He will run away. Just by my chant alone, I will defeat him. He will run."

Kamapua'a stepped forward and stood, legs apart, hands at his side, looking steadily at Makali'i. "Are you the king?" he asked. "Are you perhaps like a cliff of Po'o-mau canyon, beautiful to look at but carved into ridges by wind and rain? Who are you?"

Makali'i replied, "I am Makali'i-nui-kū-a-ka-wai-ea. I own the uplands and the lowlands. I have the lands toward the mountains and toward the sea. I am the ruling chief of Kona and soon I will be ruler of all Kaua'i. Who are you? What is your name? Can it possibly compare to mine?"

Kamapua'a replied, hinting at their past encounters in battles on O'ahu, "The turtle jumps into the sea below and holds onto the face of the rock, Makali'i-nui-kū-a-ka-wai-ea," referring to a time when Makali'i jumped into the sea to escape Kamapua'a. "My greetings to you. But it is up to you to give me my name."

Makali'i misunderstood the gibe and thought somehow that Kamapua'a was complimenting him upon his cleverness in escaping his enemy by jumping into the sea. "How well you chant my name! When I have killed Kūkona, I will save you!"

Nothing could have enraged Kamapua'a more than this taunt. "Be careful, Makali'i," Kamapua'a hissed. "You ran from me on O'ahu. I took care to let you live so you could bring the message of his defeat to 'Olopana, my uncle. Be careful, Makali'i-nui-kū-a-ka-wai-ea, my lehua flower.

> I am climbing up to reach the flower,
> Makali'i, my red lehua blossoms,
> For the sacrifice on the altar.
> I am picking the red flowers,
> I am dividing them,
> My red lehua flowers, O Makali'i.

Now I am climbing down,
For I have selected the choicest bloom.
I am braiding a lei with them;
I am stringing them in a circle;
I have completed it, O Makaliʻi.
My lei is finished."

Makaliʻi stood as one turned to stone. The word lehua was used to mean a beloved friend or a warrior. Lehua was the islet off Niʻihau that was associated with the setting sun and therefore death. A lehua was the term given to the first man to die in battle, who was sacrificed on the winner's altar. None of these meanings meant anything good to him.

Kamapuaʻa continued.

"The sea is destroying the sands of Kahalahala,
The sea of Hanalei is roaring,
The sea of Hāʻena is shallow
While the sea of Ka-lalau breaks over the land.
The spray of the sea flies up,
And my wind and cloud forms appears,
O Makaliʻi-nui-kū-a-ka-wai-ea,
Small clouds, large clouds,
Tall clouds, and short clouds
And the large cloud standing close to heaven.
That heaven is furious because of you,
O Makaliʻi-nui-kū-a-ka-wai-ea.
Your land is now mine,
The whole of Kauaʻi has become mine."

By this time Makaliʻi knew who Kamapuaʻa was. He replied, "Are you then the great hog? Is this your name?"

Kamapuaʻa answered, "Yes, it is I, Kamapuaʻa." He smiled but Makaliʻi shuddered when he saw it.

"Defeated, there is no way for me to escape," he said, letting his club fall from his hand. "There is no place to hide in the uplands, no place in the lowlands, no place toward the east or the west. There is not even a bunch of grass where I can hide. I am your prisoner."

Kamapua'a thought for a time. He had always let Makali'i go free since he had promised his grandmother to let Makali'i live. He was aware, however, that both Kūkona and Lima-loa were at his shoulders, wondering what Kamapua'a would do.

Kamapua'a said, "You will not be killed if you are able to chant one of the songs in my honor, one of my mele inoa."

Makali'i protested. "I do not know any of your chants."

Kamapua'a said, with some heat, twirling his war club menacing, "Can't you think of one?"

Makali'i closed his eyes, praying for inspiration. He began to chant and Kamapua'a relaxed his hand and his war club rested its point on the ground. The chant was of medium length and when it was done, Makali'i simply looked at him and said, "What of me?"

But Kamapua'a was still angry. "You will not be saved by one mele. You must chant another one."

Once again the gods came to the rescue of Makali'i and he chanted. It was a long chant but correct and Kamapua'a leaned comfortably against his war club and nodded encouragingly.

When the chant was over, Makali'i said, "What of me?"

"You are free," Kamapua'a said. "First, however, you must turn your kingdom over to Kūkona."

Makali'i turned to his warriors and told them the kingdom of Kona was now at an end and their new chief was Kūkona, the highest chief of the land.

"Now where shall I go?" asked Makali'i. "Perhaps you will give me a piece of land for myself and my daughter."

Kamapua'a said, "Why don't you sail to Kahiki and live there?"

"No, I will never live there," Makali'i replied, "for there are too many seas to cross. I will not leave Kaua'i."

"Go back to O'ahu and seek land from your former friends," Kamapua'a offered.

Makali'i shook his head. "I can never return to O'ahu."

"Well, then," Kamapua'a said, "go up to the mountains and live where the tī plant, the pala fern and hāpu'u tree fern are plentiful. Let your daughter marry the son of Kūkona. Then will Kaua'i be a peaceful island swimming in the sea."

Makali'i looked at Kūkona.

Kūkona replied, "Yes."

Makaliʻi turned and proceeded towards the mountains and those who revered him followed him. There along the banks of the Kōkeʻe stream, he made his home and lived with all his people.

The island now belonged to Kūkona. He divided the island among his friends. Lima-loa took the ahupuaʻa of Mānā but Kamapuaʻa wanted nothing. He slung his war club Ka-hiki-kolo over his shoulder and strode away.

> Kamapuaʻa, pig child,
> The hog that roots up the land
> Whose hand seizes the war club
> Standing on the island of Kauaʻi.
> Your name, make answer,
> The prize pig of the heavens!

Pele ame Kamapua'a

CHRISTINE FAYE '01

Pele and Kamapua'a
Pele ame Kamapua'a

Kamapua'a strolled along the banks of Hulā-'ia river. He was on his way to Ka-lalau but he was in no hurry to get there. The war between the Kona and Puna kingdoms was over. Makali'i had ceded to Kūkona. Ka-nāe-kapu-lani, Makali'i's daughter, had married Mano-ka-lani-pō, Kūkona's son. Their son would inherit the island as one kingdom. His friend Lima-loa had been given the ahupua'a of Mānā and had moved there. Kamapua'a had turned his wives, Kukui-lau-mānienie and Kukui-lau-hanahana, into stones, for he was tired of them. Now he was alone and bored. The sky was cloudless, the sun sharp, the wind listless, and the dust stirred up by his feet clogged even his eyes. He was hot, tired, and dusty. He strolled along the river bank, looking for a pool where he could swim.

He heard the waterfall before he saw it as it fell into a wide pool deep and wide enough for swimming. He could stand under the falls itself, letting the water massage his shoulders. He put down his weapons, the great war club carved from a branch of the trunkless koa tree of Ka-hiki-kolo, the spear of kauila wood from Pu'u-kā-pele, and his dagger of koai'e wood from Koai'e valley itself. He began to loosen his malo but stopped when he saw a woman come out from behind the waterfall.

She paused beneath the cascade, water flowing through her red hair and across her shoulders. She was lovely, Kamapua'a thought. He was no longer bored. Here was a game worth playing!

He moved to the edge of the cliff overlooking the falls where his image would be reflected in the water. He noticed when the woman saw his reflection she went completely still. When she looked up at him, a shiver of excitement jolted through him. This was a woman worthy of his attention, a woman his equal, and all the more desirable for that.

The woman looked up at the man standing at the brow of the cliff. He was tall, she noted, broad-shouldered, slim-waisted, long-legged, muscular, an athlete of some kind. Usually her heart beat a little faster at the sight of such an attractive man. Not this time, she noted. There was something odd about him, the way he stood, the way he stared at her. She looked closer. He had hair over much of his body, unusual for a man, thick, black, bristly hair. Then Pele laughed. She knew who and what he was.

Kamapua'a recognized her in that laugh. This was Pele-honua-mea, who had set her homeland on fire, who was fleeing her sister, and who, when Kamapua'a looked carefully around him, was alone.

"'Anoa'i 'oe," he called out. "Greetings to you."

Pele replied, "Go on your way. This is no place for you."

Kamapuaʻa smiled. "Nor is it a place for you, there in the water," he returned.

"I remember you," Pele said, her reddened eyes glaring.

> "You are Kamapuaʻa,
> The pig son of Hina and her husband.
> Whose nose is pierced by a ring,
> Whose tail wags behind him.
> Answer to your name, Kamapuaʻa!"

Her words stung like insects. Kamapuaʻa's blood warmed. He was more than eager now to trade insult for insult with this woman, to anger her as she angered him. "Now I know you," he said. "You are Pele who is careless with her fire sticks.

> It is Pele who teases the pig,
> But it is her nose that is pierced
> Pierced by love,
> Pele grunts and groans,
> Looking for the pig-man by the river.
> Yes, Pele, keep on teasing!"

Pele swam across the pool and picked up her skirt where she had carelessly thrown it on the grass. She did not like this hog man, she wanted nothing to do with him. She refused to answer him. Kamapuaʻa was angered by her silence. He chanted,

> "Who went to the heights of ʻĀipō-nui,
> What food did she eat?
> Food fit only for birds,
> ʻŌhelo berries, bird food,
> Nothing like the food
> I offer you."

Pele laughed scornfully. She left the pool, tying her skirt about her, and stooped to gather up her belongings.

Grunting "Hu! hu! hu!" Kamapuaʻa grabbed her around the waist and pulled her to him. She fought him. She scratched his arms with her fingernails. She kicked back against his legs. She knew what he wanted and she would never give it to him willingly. She bit his hand and felt his blood trickle warmly down her body. He flung her to the ground but before he could pin her, she scrambled away and ran.

When he caught up to her, Kamapuaʻa caught her by her shoulders and her knees and raised her above his head. It was a deadly move in lua, the martial art whose purpose was to break bones. He could bend her so that her back broke. He could throw her to the ground in such a way that her neck would snap. He could, and did, kneel down and pin her to the ground with his great weight. Still Pele fought, turning, twisting, kicking, scratching.

Both Pele and Kamapuaʻa were startled at hearing a great burst of laughter. A woman stood near them, gusts of laughter shaking her body.

Kamapuaʻa saw a woman who looked like Pele, red-haired, straight-backed, lovely as the full moon. Pele saw her sister, Kapo-ʻula-kinaʻu.

Kapo-ʻula-kinaʻu laughed again. "Such goings on!" she teased.

Kamapuaʻa growled. He fumbled at Pele's skirt.

Kapo-ʻula-kinaʻu laughed again. "Tell me, warrior," she said, "why do you choose a woman who wants nothing to do with you?"

"Why not?" Kamapuaʻa grunted.

"Because an unwilling partner is of no use to anyone," Kapo-ʻula-kinaʻu replied. "Better to choose one who wants you."

"And who would that be?" Kamapuaʻa snarled. "You?"

Kapo-ʻula-kinaʻu smiled broadly. "Of course," she said. "That is, if you are man enough for me."

"I am man enough and more," Kamapuaʻa boasted.

"I wonder," Kapo-ʻula-kinaʻu said. "I see you forcing an unwilling woman. A good lover has no lack of companions. That tells me you are not man enough for a willing woman. You are a weakling where it matters, perhaps."

Kamapuaʻa, stung by the challenge, rose to his feet and moved toward Kapo-ʻula-kinaʻu. Pele lost no time scrambling to her feet and ran away. Kamapuaʻa paid no attention. "Are you that woman?" he asked. "If so, I will show you what a man is."

Once again Kapo-ʻula-kinaʻu's laugh rang out. To Kamapuaʻa's ears, it promised wonders beyond imagination. "Come to me," he commanded.

"No, catch me, if you can," Kapo-'ula-kina'u said and ran toward Wai-lua. Kamapua'a ran after her. She remained easily just out of his reach. She could travel like the wind and her feet soared above the path. Kamapua'a, although a strong warrior, soon was winded and his feet were like stones, getting heavier and heavier at each step. Only Kapo-'ula-kina'u's laughter kept him running after her but soon her laughter was like the faintly heard cry of an 'ūlili bird, the wandering tattler's cry drowned in the ocean's roar. Then the only sound was the pounding in his ears.

He returned to the Hulā-'ia pond. Pele was not there. He thought of following her but decided to continue on his interrupted journey. Kamapua'a strolled along the path, in no hurry to get to Ka-lalau. He had fallen in love. Her name was Pele-honua-mea. Her name was Kapo-'ula-kina'u. He loved them both.

"We are not done with each other yet, Pele and Kapo," he said aloud. "We will meet again."

He was no longer bored. Puffy clouds covered the hot sun and Unulau, the trade wind, fanned him. "Oh, yes," he said, "we will meet again!"

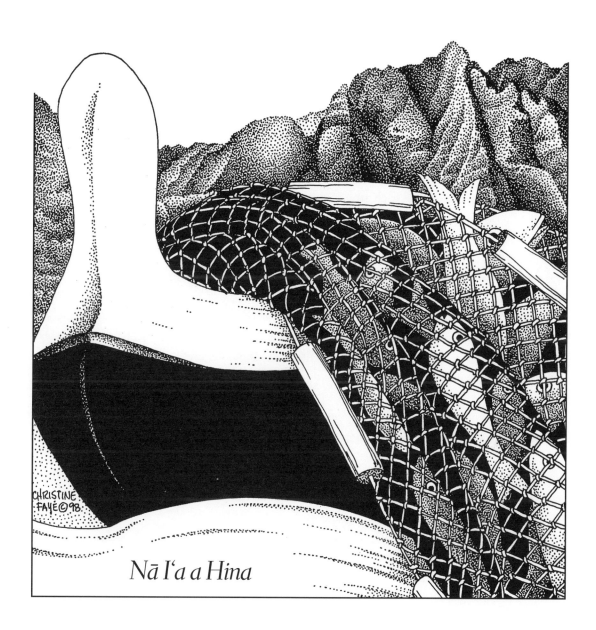

Nā Iʻa a Hina

HINA'S FISH
Nā I'a a Hina

KAMAPUA'A STOOD BESIDE NĀ-KEIKI-O-NĀ'IWI, the two rock formations half-way along Kalou trail that led from Alaka'i swamp into Ka-lalau valley. The sun was high overhead and below him the ocean sparkled. Scattered here and there he saw several kialua, the long, light, swift canoes preferred by Hina. The canoes were, he noted, in the long feeding grounds as well as in the short feeding grounds. The canoes sat low in the water, full of fish. Fishermen were still pulling in their nets and Kamapua'a counted each silvery gleam of fish caught in the mesh as the net came in over the gunwales.

Several hours earlier as Kamapua'a and his friend Kōwe'a had come up the trail from Wai-mea they had passed a lone traveler who had told them Hina's fishing crew was preparing to set out. Hina was the konohiki chiefess of Ka-lalau valley. Wai-lī-nu'u, Hina's head fisherman, had promised a plentiful catch.

Kamapua'a was pleased, for he needed a supply of both sun-dried and salted fish. He planned to sail to the south and return to the fabled islands of Kahiki and he needed food for the voyage. He was sure he would get all the fish he needed. Hina was his mother and she would be generous. He set off happily down the path.

He reached the beach just as the fishing canoes hissed up onto the sand. Kamapua'a leaned against the head fisherman's canoe and ordered Wai-lī-nu'u, "Give me some fish. If you don't, you will be killed. Death shall be your fate today and you will be food for maggots tomorrow."

Wai-lī-nu'u saw a large, muscled man covered with short bristling hair from his toes to his head. He seemed a loutish type, more hog than man and Wai-lī-nu'u was not impressed. "You are asking for two things," Wai-lī-nu'u replied, "some fish and my death. I will give you neither."

Kamapua'a demanded, "Give me some fish."

Wai-lī-nu'u responded, "Why don't you dive down into the sea and catch your own? These belong to Hina."

Kamapua'a glared and grinned. Wai-lī-nu'u thought for a moment that his teeth were really tusks, curling and sharp-tipped, ready to rip and tear unprotected flesh. Wai-lī-nu'u turned his back and began issuing orders for the care of the fish that filled his canoes.

Kamapua'a pushed his war club into the sand and leaned back on it. "I shall stay here and see that the fish are properly cleaned," he said to Kōweʻa. "You go find Hina. Tell her, 'Here comes your son. He has come for some fish for himself.'"

Kōweʻa found Hina sitting beside two young women in the shade of a milo tree. They were weaving lauhala mats. Kōweʻa delivered his message.

"You lie," Hina told Kōweʻa. "I have no other son but Kahiki-honua-kele still living. One of my sons was killed by Pele on far off Hawaiʻi. Another hung himself. Kahiki-honua-kele is the only one who is left. I don't know where this fellow you speak of comes from. I suppose he's heard about our great catch of fish and has come with a deceiving story to get himself some fish. He won't get any from me. Go back and tell him that."

Kōweʻa returned with Hina's message. Kamapuaʻa's anger flared. "I see I must go myself," he muttered. "When she sees me, she will recognize me."

Kamapuaʻa, however, did not know how much he had changed since his mother had seen him last. He had been younger, less hairy, less muscled, less like a boar than now. He did not realize that she truly thought him dead.

As Kamapuaʻa approached Hina's house, she turned away and ignored him.

"Am I supposed to converse with your back?" he asked. "I was happy as I came down the trail from the mountains to see your fleet and their great catch of fish. Hina, let me have some fish."

Hina remained silent.

After a few moments, Kamapuaʻa went on, "I came in search of my parents and now I find that my mother is mean and stingy. Where is my father? Where is my older brother? They are unkind not to come and greet me."

Once again, Hina said not a word, hoping this stranger would go away.

"Hina, I have come for some fish. Don't be unkind. It is your son who greets you."

"You are no son of mine," she muttered. "Go away."

The two young women with Hina were listening with interest to Kamapuaʻa's pleading. They were the wives of Kahiki-honua-kele. One of them touched Hina on the shoulder and said, "Say, Hina, what if this is really your son?"

Hina said, "I have no other son than your husband on Kauaʻi. If you two wish to give him some fish, you may do so."

The young women whispered to each other and composed their faces to hide the mischievous desire to teach this stranger better manners.

"Come with us," one young woman said. "We will go in our canoe and we will show you our fish."

They led Kamapua'a down to the beach and into a canoe. The women paddled north along the cliffs until they reached the entrance to Ka-ao-mao cave. Waves washed in and out of the opening creating dangerous side currents but the women dug their paddles deep into the water and the canoe sped into the opening. A trickling waterfall fell through a hole in the roof. Shafts of sunlight dimly lit the interior.

"There," said one of his guides, pointing to a huge dark shape, "there is our fish. Spear it and it is yours!"

Kamapua'a stood and threw his spear. It hit the dark shape and gouged out a piece. Only then he realized the shape was a rock shaped like a shark and not a great white shark. The two women laughed and laughed, their peals of laughter echoing from wall to wall.

When Kamapua'a left the cave, he was alone. He returned to Hina, sitting under the milo tree. With the last shreds of his patience, he repeated, "Hina, give me some fish."

Hina covered her mouth with her hand, the sign of refusal.

Kamapua'a sat in front of her. She started to her feet but Kamapua'a gestured her down and, after a brief look at his fierce eyes, she sank back on her heels. "You do not believe I am your son," he said. "I do not understand your refusal. Once, long ago, when we lived in Kalihi on O'ahu, you took me when you went fishing for crabs. You had a calabash to hold the crabs, wrapped in its carrying net and there was a cord tied to it. You used that cord to tie the calabash to a rock while we fished. Something pulled on the rope and it was broken and the calabash floated away. You went running in pursuit of the calabash but the breaking seas broke the strings of the net and the calabash filled with water and sank. We were alone, Hina. No one else was there."

Hina remembered that day. Why did she think her son had had something to do with that calabash getting free? He was always mischievous. She stole a look at the man in front of her, trying to take away the beard to see the face below. Suddenly she realized that this was indeed her youngest son whom she thought dead. She was frightened at the way she had just treated him, refusing to share her fish with him. Already the thundering look of anger filled his face with blackness. She leaped to her feet and rushed into her house.

Kamapua'a waited for her return.

Hina silently tore a hole in the back wall of the house and ran to where her husband Kahiki'ula and her son Kahiki-honua-kele were preparing kava for the coming evening. She told them of the warrior waiting for her outside the house. "This is Kamapua'a," she said breathlessly. "He has arrived here, back from the dead. He is angry with me."

The three looked unhappily at one another. Kamapua'a, when angry, never forgot an insult until it had been avenged.

"You must go and greet him properly," Kahiki-'ula said. "Perhaps he will forgive you."

"You must come, too," she insisted.

"You go and we will see how he treats you. Then we will come," Kahiki'ula replied.

So Hina walked back to where Kamapua'a waited for her. As soon as she could see him, she began to chant.

> "Auwē, my son, it is raining!
> I have no gifts to offer you,
> No way to appease your anger,
> There is only the heaven above,
> Weeping, for my tears are like the rain.
> It is raining; I am wet,
> My body is wet with the rain.
> My son of the tall cliff of Ka-lalau!"

She knelt at Kamapua'a's feet and when he would not look at her, she stretched out along the ground. He stepped over her and sat down on her back, a gesture of unforgiveness. He was angry, for he still had no fish.

Kahiki-'ula, peering around the corner of a house, recognized the warrior sitting on his wife. "That's the man that saved me," he whispered to Kahiki-honua-kele, "after I was defeated by Kūkona."

"He's the one who saved me after I was struck down by Lima-loa," said Kahiki-honua-kele. "I did not recognize him as my brother."

"We must ask him to stop being angry,"Kahiki-'ula said. The two walked swiftly to Kamapua'a and lay down on the ground beside Hina.

The pig-man snorted, stood, and deliberately stepped on each of them, a sign of great contempt, and walked toward the beach. He was very angry but he had not yet decided to kill them, although they deserved to die for insulting him.

His mother ran after him, wailing piteously. She chanted his name songs, she pleaded with him to forgive her. He ignored her and continued walking. At last she stopped and, with an agonizing cry that made Kamapua'a turn to look at her, pulled off her clothing and crawled, nude, toward him. It was an act of utter abandonment, of abject submission, the last desperate cry for forgiveness. Either he pardoned her, or killed her, or she would kill herself.

Shamed, Kamapua'a rushed to pick up her clothes and draped them around her. She clung to him, weeping.

After a time, he said gently, "Hina, give me some fish."

"Take all you want," she said. "My fish are yours."

"Why did you not recognize me?" he asked.

Hina explained the number of years that had passed since she had last seen him, hardly more than a boy and not the seasoned warrior she now held in her arms. She told him of the report of his death. Of course she thought him dead. He, she said softly, had never sent word that he was alive. Kamapua'a laughed then, forgiving her and through her his father and brother.

Then he thought of fish and of the insult of the fisherman Wai-lī-nu'u. He said, "Your fisherman must die, however, for he told me that I must dive down into the sea to get my fish."

"Yes," Hina replied.

Kamapua'a twirled his war club once and brought it down sharply on Wai-lī-nu'u's head. Then he threw the body to the sharks. He asked Hina to dry certain fish and salt certain others. After a few weeks, Kamapua'a said farewell to his mother for the last time. Then Kamapua'a and Kōwe'a carried their bundles of preserved fish over the mountains to Wai-mea. There they climbed aboard a double-hulled voyaging canoe and sailed to return to the fabled atolls and islands of Kahiki.

Ka He'e Nalu 'ana ma Wai-lua

CHRISTINE FAYE ©98

Surfing at Wai-lua
Ka Heʻe Nalu ʻana ma Wai-lua

AS THEY CAME TO THE BROW OF THE RIDGE, just after passing Poli-ʻahu heiau and making a brief offering there, Kapo-ʻula-kinaʻu raised her hand. Like a band of geese, the nine young women for whom she had promised to find husbands and Ka, brother of Kapo-ʻula-kinaʻu, gathered around her, wondering why she had stopped and why she was staring down the broad expanse of the Wai-lua river. There were no canoes on it, no fish jumped to break the water surface, that great mirror reflecting only the few clouds over head.

But Kapo-ʻula-kinaʻu was looking beyond the river mouth, beyond a beach of dazzling white sand, the beach of Alio where the gods had created the first man and woman. Beyond Alio was the sea, a sea that did not rise and fall without breaking. There were crests to these waves, the long-back billows that followed one after another. The spray broke in masses in the sea. This was a large surf, the surf that brings combers to carry the daring rider on an exhilarating ride, swooping and sliding down the face, into and through tunnels formed by the breakers, with unimagined speed and always danger waited for the rider's skill to falter. It took skill to catch a wave on a long surfboard of koa wood, to launch oneself firmly and then to stand, balancing with one's feet, digging in with one's toes, and ride the ferocious monster from farthest Kahiki, from the edges of the sea to ride safely to land. There were many accidents, broken bones, torn flesh, even death was to be found in these waves. It was a sport in which women could excel for it did not take sheer muscular strength, it took skill, balance, a feeling for the force of the surging water, knowing how to stay out of the breaking wave, sliding along its smooth surface just before the break. It was Kapo-ʻula-kinaʻu's sport. Almost as if she had sprouted wings, she rushed down the trail, her companions like a bewildered school of akule following in her wake.

The clear sound of a singing stone being struck once, twice, pealed as they passed.

"Our arrival is being announced," said Ka.

"All the better," replied Kapo-ʻula-kinaʻu. "Little need for looking for the chief, he or she will come looking for us."

In moments, they were at the sea, and Kapo-ʻula-kinaʻu watched the men and women riding the surf. There was a multitude of surf riders. Some rode the left breaking waves, others the right breaking waves. The sea ran high, the waves were big and offered tremendous rides for the brave.

This was the surf of Maka'iwa, where hundreds of years before Hina-a-ulu-ā surfed and married Mo'ikeha, the traveler from Rai'ātea far, far to the south. This is where their granddaughter Ka-'ili-lau-o-ke-koa surfed with her friends. This is where the chiefs from all the islands came to demonstrate their abilities as well as the beauty of their bodies, for admiring eyes compared, approved or scorned what they saw. Kapo-'ula-kina'u scanned the surfers and with some satisfaction found there were eight young men who surfed together in a group and, unlike some of the others, did not surf in pairs with lovely young women. Good, there were eight men, she had nine women to marry, now all she needed was the ninth.

A voice spoke to her, "E welina ho'i 'oe, my greetings to you."

Kapo-'ula-kina'u turned. She saw a man who was good looking and whose bearing was regal from head to foot. There was nothing about him to offend her eyes for there were no scars or blemishes anywhere on him.

"And my greetings to you," Kapo-'ula-kina'u returned.

"My name is Kau-maka-a-mano. Let me welcome you to Wai-lua-nui-a-ho'āno." He was soft spoken and courteous.

"I am made welcome, indeed," she replied.

"Do you surf?" Kau-maka-a-mano asked. "I see you looking at the waves with hunger in your eyes."

"Indeed I do," Kapo-'ula-kina'u said. "The waves are excellent today. It is a pity I am a stranger and have no board with which to surf."

"You will use mine as long as you wish," Kau-maka-a-mano said, pointing to his board, a highly polished piece of koa, artfully molded to make the best use of the water and the weight of the surfer, eight feet high, a long board only experts could use. If he expected her to refuse such a board, he did not show it as she lifted the board easily and ran to the ocean. In moments she was out in the surf and in no time had caught a large billow and was flying towards land, her long red-tinged hair streaming out behind her like the rays of the setting sun touch the sky with red.

"She is an expert," Ka said. "I am her brother."

"And her name?"

"Kapo-'ula-kina'u of the red feather cape dotted with black specks, and I am Ka."

"You are strangers here," Kau-maka-a-mano said, "but you are most welcome." He looked attentively at the nine young women surrounding Ka. One in particular caught his fancy and for the first time in his young life, Kau-maka-a-mano wondered what it was to live for years with one woman, a wife, a companion, the twin of oneself. The young woman, whose name was Ka-hala-iʻa, smiled back at him and her eyes looked steadily into his. "Do you all surf, too?" he asked.

Ka-hala-iʻa laughed. "Oh, yes, but not like our chiefess Kapo-ʻula-kinaʻu."

"I can, perhaps, find boards for you to use," he offered.

"No need, I think Kapo-ʻula-kinaʻu has found some boards we can use."

Thoroughly enjoying the surfing, Kapo-ʻula-kinaʻu had not forgotten one of her important goals, finding husbands for her women. She knew she herself would not be free to seek her own love until they were settled. She had quickly moved into the center of the eight men and struck up conversation as they sat balancing on their boards, waiting for the next large wave. They did not know, of course, that Kapo-ʻula-kinaʻu could control the waves and she had willed that only small combers would come, those that rise and fall without breaking and without sufficient strength to speed a surfboard.

Kapo-ʻula-kinaʻu exclaimed, "Look at those beautiful women on the sands of Alio. Where did they come from?"

They all looked and one man said, "Perhaps they came from the uplands of Pihana-ka-lani."

"I am sure they would like to surf," Kapo-ʻula-kinaʻu said. "You should ask them. Just think what pleasure you would have if you rode two to a board, one man, one woman. One of you go with that one, another with the one over there. What do you say?"

Since there were no waves at the moment and none seemed to be showing up on the horizon, and as Kau-maka-a-mano beckoned to them to come ashore, the eight men and Kapo-ʻula-kinaʻu paddled to the beach. Kapo-ʻula-kinaʻu quickly paired them off, one man to one woman, but at the end, her friend Ka-hala-iʻa was left without a partner.

"I do not mind," Ka-hala-iʻa said. "Continue surfing yourself."

"No, no," Kapo-ʻula-kinaʻu replied. "Here is the board I borrowed and here is the man I borrowed it from. The two of you go out. I shall wait here. And then afterwards the men will take the women to their houses, just as we have paired off here. What do you say?"

Kau-maka-a-mano nodded happily and said, "Yes, what a good idea. I shall send word to my parents that we will have company this night and to prepare a feast for us." He smiled at Ka-hala-iʻa and took her out surfing on his board.

Kapo-ʻula-kinaʻu did not notice that the eight men themselves had said nothing but had looked strangely at each other. Following their chief they took their partners, plunged into the water and paddled to the surf of Makaʻiwa.

As soon as they got there, Kapo-'ula-kina'u summoned large waves and the pairs rode them, for the young women were experts in the sport. After one run in, the eight young women jumped off their boards and waded ashore. An admiring throng of men and women came with wreaths of maile and palai fern and placed them around the necks of each of these women of mystery.

Kapo-'ula-kina'u asked, "Why are you not surfing? After all, I have come to marry you to a man."

"What man?" the young woman replied. "Is a farmer a man?"

"A farmer?" Kapo-'ula-kina'u asked. "A commoner?"

"That is what he said," the young woman replied. "He said he could not take me home with him tonight as he has only a farmer's hovel. He does not like me, that one." She shrugged her shoulders and mingled with the admiring women and men who were offering them refreshments.

"And you?" Kapo-'ula-kina'u asked a second woman. "Why are you not surfing?"

"I am looking for a man," she replied. "That one is only a fisherman. He only has a lean-to on the beach. He cannot take me home with him, he says. It is just as well."

One by one she asked the other six young women. Each said the man they were with had found some excuse or another to refuse to bring them to their homes that night. Each of the young women had been rejected. Kapo-'ula-kina'u was furious. Only Kau-maka-a-mano and Ka-hala-i'a were still surfing together and it seemed to her practiced eye that they would continue their newly found friendship. But first, Kapo-'ula-kina'u had something to do. She beckoned to Kau-maka-a-mano and he obligingly caught a wave, Ka-hala-i'a standing tall and magnificent in front of him.

"Allow me to borrow your board," Kapo-'ula-kina'u said.

"Of course," Kau-maka-a-mano replied and led Ka-hala-i'a to where her sisters were resting under the coconut trees.

Kapo-'ula-kina'u paddled out. "Listen to me," she called out to the eight men as she came into their midst.

"We are listening," came the reply.

"I make a bet with you. I can ride a bigger surf than any of you safely to shore."

The men looked doubtfully at her. Sometimes there were big waves, so big that only the most daring of athletes dared to take them. "We cannot bring waves to us; we must wait for them," one replied.

"Nonetheless," Kapo-'ula-kina'u said. "I challenge you."

No man could resist a bet. There was not a one of them that had not bet on the outcome of a sports event, a boxing match, a javelin toss, ti leaf boats in a river race. "What shall we wager?" one said.

"Our bones!" Kapo-'ula-kina'u said.

Before the men could object, Kapo-'ula-kina'u caused a huge wave to come in from the deep ocean. "Let us ride this one!" she called and launched herself onto the comber. She rose to her feet, her hair blowing out behind her. The eight men were also standing. The nine of them swept down the comber's face, flipped away and paddled out once again.

"We were all together on that one," one man said.

"Indeed," said Kapo-'ula-kina'u. "But the day is not over yet."

She caused another, even larger wave to loom above them. Once again the nine caught the wave but it was far bigger than the men were used to and they struggled and two fell. Kapo-'ula-kina'u rode triumphantly the whole course of the wave to the beach. Kau-maka-a-mano was waiting for her.

Kau-maka-a-mano said, for these were his men and he was worried, "Two fell. You have won your bet."

"Not yet," Kapo-'ula-kina'u replied. "My bet was with all eight. Do not interfere with me, chief." Her eyes blazed and Kau-maka-a-mano nodded.

Ka-hala-i'a took his hand as Kapo-'ula-kina'u headed out to sea once again. "She has strange powers," Ka-hala-i'a said, "and it is safer not to interfere with her when she is in one of these moods. Those men, by rejecting my sisters, insulted her. She will be revenged."

"And you, what powers do you have?" he murmured and allowed himself to be led to a leafy shaded seat to watch Kapo-'ula-kina'u.

Kapo-'ula-kina'u resumed her place in the middle of the eight men. She sat on her board and untied her belt of pōhuehue vine. Taking hold of one end of it, she whipped it into the ocean, first on one side, then on the other, and back and forth and again and again, chanting:

> "Rise up, rise up, great waves from Kahiki!
> Powerful curling waves,
> Rise up, the pōhuehue calls you
> Arise, long raging surf!"

"Now, ride this one!" Kapo-'ula-kina'u called as a long, high wave came speeding toward them. "This is no wave, this is a mountain! Let each of you try his skill! Go ahead, ride shoreward!" Kapo-'ula-kina'u laughed and it seemed to those on the shore that lightning flashed about her and that she was clothed by the phosphorescent sea as she rode this gigantic wave. In a moment the onlookers realized that this monstrous wave would not harmlessly hiss onto shore but would rage far up over the land. They ran towards the mountains, hoping to escape.

No sooner had the eight men caught the wave than they were pulled beneath the water. There they were pummeled by the churning water and pounded onto the bottom and ground along the rocks until they, too, became stones, each marked with the image of the man he once was. The rocks washed along the ocean bottom and clung onto the rock wall of Hikina-a-ka-lā heiau.

These eight rocks are there to this day. They are known as the pae kiʻi, the row of images, because of the markings on them. Kapo-ʻula-kinaʻu laughed when she saw them. "It would have been better had you married my young women," she told them, but they could not hear.

Afterwards Kau-maka-a-mano led his guests to his parents' home where they were greeted and offered fine hospitality and a great feast was spread before them. At the end of it Kapo-ʻula-kinaʻu and her daughters entertained their hosts with rollicking, fun-filled hula and with solemn dances in honor of the gods. Late in the evening, Kapo-ʻula-kinaʻu turned to Kau-maka-a-mano.

"I have no gift to give you for your hospitality and your friendliness to me," she said.

"None is needed," he replied but Kapo-ʻula-kinaʻu touched him on the lips to silence him.

"I have only Ka-hala-iʻa, my daughter, to offer you. Is that agreeable to you both?" Kapo-ʻula-kinaʻu looked at Ka-hala-iʻa and a tear formed in the corner of her eye. She would soon be losing a life-long friend. Ka-hala-iʻa nodded and whispered, "Yes."

"Yes," Kau-maka-a-mano said, "if my parents approve."

The ruling chief, Mano-ka-lani-pō and his wife Nae-kapu-o-Makaliʻi smiled on their son. Mano-ka-lani-pō said, "We have heard of Kapo-ʻula-kinaʻu. And we know of her sister Pele. We are pleased that Kapo-ʻula-kinaʻu has chosen you as a son-in-law."

"That is settled, then," Kapo-ʻula-kinaʻu said. "Only one more thing to do." She took Ka-hala-iʻa's hand and kissed her gently on the forehead. "Go in peace, my daughter. Remember us. Your name is now and forever Kapo-ino-kai, Kapo of the ocean spray, in memory of our trip together from our homeland to the island of Kauaʻi. Here you must stay and I must go on. But not for a few days yet."

Kapo-ʻula-kinaʻu placed over the heads of Kau-maka-a-mano and Kapo-ino-kai the decorated tapa that symbolized their marriage. The feasting and dancing went on through the night but Kau-maka-a-mano and Kapo-ino-kai, unnoticed, crept away. Only Kapo-ʻula-kinaʻu saw them go. The tear that had been hovering in her eye slid slowly down her cheek.

Ka Make o Lohi'au

The Death of Lohiʻau
Ka Make o Lohiʻau

Ipo-noʻenoʻe, the wind that lures women to Hāʻena, blew gently across the lagoon of Kēʻē into the open sides of the hālau, a shed with coconut frond walls. It caught up the rhythmic beat of the deep-throated sharkskin drum played by Mapu, the music teacher. It gathered the sounds of the light-toned drum played by Lohiʻau and the rustle of the kaʻekeʻeke thrummed by Ka-lei-paoa. Ipo-noʻenoʻe left the hall, skirted the cliff of Makana peak, continued across the island, over the seas, to bring the sound to the ear of Pele, she who had found a home for herself and her family in the pit of Hale-maʻumaʻu, but had never found a man she could love. Pele lay on her couch, an old woman with white hair, wrinkled skin and red eyes. She listened to the Ipo-noʻenoʻe.

"There at Kēʻē," whispered the wind, "at Hāʻena on Kauaʻi, there is a school for chant and dance. Kilioe is the woman who leads the prayers to Laka, god of the dance. It is Kilioe, who feeds the great white shark that guards her pupils against error. Ka-hua-nui is there with her man Ke-koa-ola. Ka-lei-paoa is chief of the school of history and genealogy. His friend is Lohiʻau, brother of Ka-hua-nui, young, handsome, his back as straight as the cliffs, his face ruddy with health like the ʻōhelo berry. He is young, he is alone, he yearns for love, perhaps even the love of Pele." The wind whispered in her ear. "You too are alone, you too yearn for love." Chuckling to itself the wind blew eastward to greet the sun.

Pele sank into sleep, warning her sisters not to awaken her. Her spirit floated up as her breathing slowed and, following the sound of drums, sped toward their source. She stepped onto the beach at Kēʻē, young again, her flaming red hair streaming down her back, her slim supple body wrapped in a pāʻū of charcoal gray. She paused, unseen in the doorway of the hālau.

The hālau was filled with men and women listening and watching with great attention. At the far end were the three drummers Mapu, Ka-lei-paoa, and Lohiʻau. She recognized him immediately, young, strong, worthy to be consort to a goddess. Facing them were the dancers led by Kilioe and Ka-hua-nui. They were dancing the hula ʻōniu, the dance of the spinning top.

> The rustle and hum of a spinning top,
> Wild laughter and babbling of voices
> Reach the heights of Ka-iwi-kuʻi
> Stirring the Piliwale sisters from their sleep.

At first no one saw Pele as she stood in the doorway. Then a woman saw the stranger from the corner of her eye and turned to look in wonder and admiration. She had never seen a woman of such beauty and bearing. She nudged her neighbor and one by one everyone fell silent, turning to look at the red-haired woman.

"Who is she?" whispered one.

"Indeed," was the reply. "Surely not from Kaua'i. We would have heard of such a beauty."

"How did she come here?" asked another.

A shrug was the only reply.

The drumming continued as Pele began to walk toward the musicians. People fell back, opening a lane for her to pass through. She kept her eyes fixed on Lohi'au, her mind busy with plans to win him for her husband and plans to bring him from Hā'ena to Hale-ma'uma'u. The hall grew silent. First Ka-lei-paoa's drumming stopped in mid-note. Mapu fell silent, gaping with open mouth and wide eyes. Only Lohi'au, caught up in his drum's voice, continued to beat out his rhythm. The dancers, too, stopped in mid-step and turned to look at the magnificent stranger.

Ka-hua-nui, Lohi'au's sister, said to her husband Ke-koa-ola, "I do not like the look of her."

"She is beautiful," he replied.

"Indeed she is," Ka-hua-nui said, "and dangerous."

Pele stopped in front of the raised platform. Lohi'au looked up and in that instant he belonged to Pele. He could not speak, he could no longer move. He could only look and stare.

Pele reached out her hand in a pleading gesture. She began to chant and her listeners thought they had never heard such a song and listened spellbound.

> "Hanalei is beaten down by the heavy rains
> Falling from the clouds over Alaka'i swamp.
> The rain reaches Manu'a-kepa
> Where the traveler falls on slippery moss.
> Where is one to lead the newcomer safely?
> I search for one to give me life
> To bring life to me here!"

She waited for an answer. Ka-lei-paoa understood her meaning and for a moment he was jealous. A pity she had not sung to him, he thought.

In the stillness every eye was on Lohi'au, waiting his answer. No one knew who she was, no one imagined she was Pele of the volcano. Her appearance announced that she was a person of distinction, a chiefess of rank, one whom their chief Lohi'au should be privileged to offer hospitality. Yet he remained silent, his eyes fixed in awe upon the woman in front of him.

Mapu wrinkled his forehead and nodded, trying to break Lohi'au's trance. Ka-lei-paoa looked at him and winked, as though this was all a joke. They hoped to rouse him and remind him of the duties of a host. He remained mute and still. Ka-lei-paoa nudged him in his ribs. Pele smiled and chanted again.

> "I am shivering in the rain
> The wind is roaring
> No answering voice do I hear.
> There is only silence.
> I hear whispering around me
> Quick glances that quickly turn away
> I see lowered heads.
> Where is a friend for me?
> A friend? Speak!"

This song awoke Lohi'au from his rapturous dream. He rose and said, "Welcome, stranger, come, sit beside me and we will feast together. My friends shall entertain you with song and dance."

Pele seated herself on the mat-piled dais, Ka-lei-paoa having moved away to make room for her. Ka-hua-a-paoa's eyes were fixed on the stranger. It was not her beauty that held his attention but rather an aura of power, of authority, of the certainty of command. She was not for him, not now, but he sensed that there was a future for them, he and she. He was content to wait and watch.

Lohi'au, as custom demanded, asked Pele, "Who are you and who are your forebears?"

"I am of Kaua'i," she replied.

"There is no woman of Kaua'i your equal in beauty," Lohi'au said. "I have visited every part of the island and seen no one like you."

Pele shrugged. "You have undoubtedly wandered here and there over this island," she said, "but there are places you have missed. And that is where I am from."

"No, no," he protested, "you are not of Kaua'i! Tell me where are you from?"

Pele relented. He would find out soon enough and would join her when she had regained her physical body. Pele had never been so displeased to be in her spiritual form. She could not do what she longed to do! She smiled at Lohi'au and said, "I am from Puna, from the land of the sunrise, from Ha'eha'e, the eastern gate of the sun."

At that moment platters and calabashes filled with food were spread out before Pele and Lohi'au who alone remained on the platform. The musicians had inched their way off and the two were alone.

Lohi'au offered his guest a freshwater shrimp. Pele refused. "I have eaten," she said.

"How can that be?" Lohi'au said. "You have just come and you have had a long journey to get here. You must eat."

Pele pushed away his hand. "I am not hungry," she replied, "at least not for food." She looked at him boldly, not caring to hide her feelings.

Lohi'au's stomach gave a great heave. He, too, could not eat. His mind was whirling with hopes.

"I am weary from the journey," Pele said.

Lohi'au leapt to his feet and led her, not in the least unwilling, to his house. There they embraced, rubbing noses, blowing gently in each other's ears, running hands eagerly over warm flesh. He lowered her to his bed and reached to untie her pā'ū. She seized his hand and kissed him. No matter what he did or wanted to do, Pele fed him only kisses. He forgot his own need for food and drink. He forgot his duties as chief. He forgot his love of music. He forgot all the obligations that rested upon him as a host. He wanted to possess her and was enflamed with love. Pele was content.

All that night, and the following day, and another night, for three days and nights, he lay at her side. He struggled with her; she would not let him undo the knot of her pā'ū. He pleaded and still she refused, keeping him from despair only by her kisses.

Then on the third night, at the darkest part of the morning before the first light of dawn appears, Pele said to Lohi'au, "It is time for me to leave. I must go back to Puna, land of the sunrise."

"I will go with you," Lohi'au said eagerly.

"No," Pele said gently. "You must remain here. I will go home and prepare a place for us to live. When all is ready, I will send a messenger for you. If by some chance a man should come and say he was sent by me, do not go with him. If my messenger is a woman, go with her. When we are together, all I ask is to be with you for five days and five nights when we will take our fill of pleasure in one another. After that, you will be free to go with another woman."

"Never!" Loha'iu cried.

Pele laughed and prepared to leave. Lohi'au caught her in his arms but she easily slipped aside. "Not until we meet on Hawai'i," she laughed.

He fought with her and caught her arm. She raised his hand to her mouth and bit him. He grabbed his hand to stanch the blood without letting her go. He swooped down and bit her on the back of her hand. Pele's eyes glinted with anger but then she laughed, fled from the house and plunged into the ocean and was gone.

Lohi'au lay down on the bed where she had once lain but it was cold and empty. The wound where she had bitten him scabbed over and the scabs fell off until only the faint mark of her teeth remained. He stood at the doorway of his house and gazed eastward but no messenger came. Then he placed a kapu sign before his door, warning he was to be left alone. He went inside and the wondering people of Kē'ē saw him no more.

Night after night, day after day passed without a sign of Lohi'au. Ka-hua-nui and Ka-hua-a-paoa grew concerned, then became worried. Their concern grew into alarm.

"Why does he not come out?" Ka-lei-paoa asked.

"Why does he not answer us?" Ka-hua-nui asked.

"We cannot disobey his kapu sign," Ka-lei-paoa said.

"I think we can," Ka-hua-nui said, "it has been far too long since we last saw him."

She went into Lohi'au's house, brushing past the kapu sign. She called out in alarm and Ka-lei-paoa rushed to her.

Despondent, for he had been forsaken, alone, for the lovely woman had failed to send a messenger, despairing of ever seeing her again, Lohi'au had taken off his malo, tied one end around his neck and the other around a rafter, and hung himself. When Ka-hua-nui and Ka-hua-a-paoa entered, his body was still warm. Ka-lei-paoa lifted down the body of his friend.

"I shall avenge you," he swore, removing his own malo. "I shall not wear my malo again until I have revenged your death on this woman." He became one with the naked god Ka-hō-'āli'i, keeper of the two axes for carving canoes. Only when he had the eye of a sacrifice would his oath end.

Lohi'au's body was prepared for burial although it never grew cold. His friends wailed his death and mourned his passing. He was placed in a cove in the cliffs above his home.

"Do not fear," Kilioe, chiefess of the hula school, told Ka-hua-nui, "I and my sister will guard the opening of the cave. No one shall disturb his bones."

Ipo-no'eno'e, wind of Hā'ena, carried the silence of death to Pele who did not listen. In love herself, she gave instructions to her sister Hi'iaka-i-ka-poli-o-Pele to travel to Kē'ē and bring Lohi'au to Hale-ma'uma'u. Ipo-no'eno'e sighed, wept a little, and sadly flew eastward to ease her sorrow in the far reaches of the empty ocean.

Ka Papa 'Auwai a Wai-lua

The Footbridge of Wai-lua
Ka Papa 'Auwai a Wai-lua

FOR AS LONG AS ANYONE COULD REMEMBER, the mo'o Wai-lua guarded the crossing of Wai-lua river. All travelers to and from Wai-lua-nui-a-hōano, chiefs in their feathered helmets, chiefesses with feather wreaths twined in their hair, warriors, white clad priests, all the maka'āinana commoners, men and women staggering under the loads of provisions needed to supply the voracious appetites at Wai-lua-nui-a-hōano, everyone had to cross the river in this one spot.

Wai-lua had chosen her place well. Her crossing was just above the thundering Wai-ehu waterfall where the waters from Ka-wai-kini flowed a hundred feet over a lip of black lava into a deep, turbulent pool. Between this pool and the river mouth, the cliffs were steep and the water was deep; no easy place for the constant to and fro out of and into Wai-lua-nui-a-hōano. Above Wai-ehu were countless streams with round moss-covered rocks and sudden flash floods from unseen rain storms thousands of feet above in the swamp of Alaka'i.

Each morning Wai-lua knelt on a flat rock at the river's edge, and washed her hair in the cold water. She would break off a stalk of ginger and squeeze its juice into her tresses and scrub and rinse. Then she would take her bamboo comb and contentedly untangle her hair until it shone in the sunlight. Then and only then would she treat travelers wishing to cross the river with some politeness. Wai-lua had saved the long planks from the side of the canoe, which had brought her from the forgotten lands of Kāne-huna-moku. If asked and if she were in an accommodating mood, Wai-lua would slide a plank across the river just above the falls and the traveler would walk safely across. There was no crossing the river without Wai-lua's plank for the water was swift and the river wide and the moss thick and slippery. To lose one's footing meant being caught in the swift current and flung over the thundering waterfall. Few survived such a fall.

Only ka papa 'auwai a Wai-lua, Wai-lua's footbridge, could bring a traveler from one side of the river to the other safely and dry.

However, crossing the river was never as simple and carefree as a traveler might wish. If Wai-lua was not finished combing her lovely dark hair and was interrupted by a call, she would slide the plank across. When the traveler reached the center, Wai-lua would grab the end of the plank and shake it back and forth. The traveler would stagger, throw up his hands to balance himself, causing any bundles he was carrying to be swept over the falls, soon to be followed by the person himself.

86

Wai-lua did not care whether the person survived the fall; she never looked. So it became the custom to wait until mid-morning and, once safely on land again, to leave Wai-lua a little offering in thanks for her service. People quickly learned that she never forgot a rude word or a cheap payment and the next time such a person crossed the river, Wai-lua would shake the plank and the hapless one would fall into the swift water.

So it was until one day, early in the morning, Hiʻiaka-i-ka-poli-o-Pele, her friend Wahine-ʻōmaʻo and her companion Pāʻū-o-palaʻe, came to the banks of the river. Hiʻiaka was anxious to continue her journey for she had been sent by her sister Pele to bring the Hāʻena chief Lohiʻau back to Hale-maʻumaʻu and already she was very late. The three women had risen early from their landing place at Hanamāʻulu bay and were eager to be on their way.

In the mountains there had been heavy rains during the night and swift water, covering all but the largest rocks, flowed brown and seething over the falls. Mist filled the air and quickly covered the three women with dampness.

Hiʻiaka saw a young woman kneeling on a rock on the other side of the river. Hiʻiaka called out, "How do we cross this river?"

Wai-lua looked up, but immediately returned to washing her hair. She remained silent.

Hiʻiaka, containing her rising anger, chanted a warning to the moʻo:

> "Clear is Wai-ʻaleʻale in the calm day,
>   Visible next to Ka-wai-kini peak
>   Which reaches far into the sky.
>   The stream-crossing plank is missing,
>   An obstacle on our way to Nounou mountain
>   And the broad plain of Kapaʻa beyond.
>   Where is the plank? Answer!
>   No voice reaches this side of the river."

Wai-lua was irritated at the intrusion. "When Wai-lua is ready," she answered, "she will send across her plank. You will have to wait." She returned to the pleasures of washing her hair.

"We can't wait all day," Wahine-ʻōmaʻo snapped.

The moʻo shrugged her shoulders. "All right," she said, scarcely concealing her irritation. She slid the plank across the river.

Wahine-‘ōma‘o strode onto the plank and began to march across. As she reached the middle, Wai-lua began to shake the plank. To Wai-lua's surprise, Wahine-‘ōma‘o did not lose her balance and fall, wailing, into the water. Instead, she rushed forward along the plank and leaped to the safety of the bank. Then she grabbed the mo‘o by the wrists, pulling her arms painfully behind her back.

"Come ahead," Wahine-‘ōma‘o called across the river. "All is well."

Hi‘iaka crossed carefully. Wai-lua lunged forward, pulling away from Wahine-‘ōma‘o's grasp, and seized the plank and pushed it as hard as she could. The plank slid away from the bank. Hi‘iaka ran forward and leaped, landing heavily on the shore. The plank, caught by the heaving water, pointed downwards and disappeared over the edge of the waterfall. Pā‘ū-o-pala‘e was alone on the far bank.

"That is a cruel trick," Hi‘iaka said angrily. "Is this how you treat strangers to your land?"

They glared at each other angrily. As she stared Hi‘iaka recognized the woman before her as a mo‘o, a member of the detested lizard clan. She had been slowed in her journey to fetch Lohi‘au by constant delays caused by mo‘o and she had no patience with them. She raised her hand to destroy the mo‘o before her.

But in that same moment Wai-lua recognized that Hi‘iaka was no ordinary traveler. She knew she faced her doom. With a squeak of terror, Wai-lua transformed herself into a small gecko and scurried over the edge of the bank and made her way upstream to Ka-welo-wai cave deep underwater.

Hi‘iaka began to follow her but Wahine-‘ōma‘o said, "We have no time to waste on such as she. What about Pā‘ū-o-pala‘e?" She gestured across the river where Pā‘ū-o-pala‘e waited with the bundles of Hi‘iaka's possessions.

Hi‘iaka looked down into the pool at the foot of Wai-ehu and saw the plank eddying about in several splintered pieces. She studied the river, noting the large rocks that even in this spate kept their heads above the water. Hi‘iaka concentrated and with the special powers given her by her sister Pele, goddess of the volcano, she found one large rock after another deep in the riverbed. These moved beside the large stones until, from one bank to the other, there was a row of stepping stones.

"Come across!" Hi‘iaka called to Pā‘ū-o-pala‘e. So Pā‘ū-o-pala‘e was the first to cross the river on stepping stones so large and so close to one another that even in flood times, a traveler could step from one stone to the other without getting wet.

Hi‘iaka and her two companions hurried away for they were late. It was a long time later that a little gecko crept out of Ka-welo-wai cave, looking fearfully in all directions. She assumed her human form but, since her plank was lost, and travelers could come and go across the river on Hi'iaka's stepping stones, there was nothing left for her to do. She was always looking down the road in fear that Hi'iaka would return. She became nervous and her hair lost its luster. It was more than she could bear.

Wai-lua plunged into the river and as far as anyone knows, she returned to her homeland, Kāne-huna-moku. She no longer can be seen by the banks of the river combing her hair. She no longer slides her plank from one bank to the other for a traveler to cross. Even the trail itself is now forgotten and no one crosses the river by way of ka papa 'auwai a Wai-lua.

Ka Wahine Hākeno a Ke-ālia

©CHRISTINE FAYE 9?

THE SICK WOMAN OF KE-ĀLIA
Ka Wahine Hākeno a Ke-ālia

THE SUN HAD ALREADY HIDDEN behind the steep ridges of Maka-leha when Hiʻiaka-i-ka-poli-o-Pele, her friend Wahine-ʻōmaʻo and her companion Pāʻū-o-palaʻe came to the edge of Ke-ālia ahupuaʻa. They rested a moment, looking at the broad beach, the wide mouthed valley and the trail disappearing over another rise going toward the high peaks above Anahola. Hiʻiaka was tired. She had been a long time on the road, sent to Kauaʻi by her sister Pele to bring Lohiʻau to Hawaiʻi. There had been many battles along the way, many delays, and Hiʻiaka felt that being at rest in one place for a long time would be welcome.

Wahine-ʻomaʻo looked sourly on the view. There were a few houses scattered here and there but most of them were far up the valley, a long trudge in the gathering dusk. "Where are we going to spend the night?" she demanded. "And what will we eat?"

"There is a house tucked in behind that grove of hala trees by the beach," Pāʻū-o-palaʻe said. It was a small house and they could see a man sitting in front of it huddled over a fire. His body was slumped, shoulders down, knees bent awkwardly, hanging head, a man laden with sorrow.

Hiʻiaka sighed. "Is there nowhere else?" she asked.

"Not that I can see," Wahine-ʻōmaʻo replied, "unless you want a long walk in the dark."

"At least we will be protected from the night wind," Pāʻū-o-palaʻe said.

"I don't know," Hiʻiaka said. "He is obviously in pain of some sort."

Wahine-ʻōmaʻo looked at Hiʻiaka with searching eyes. It was obvious to her that her friend was tired and discouraged. Better to go forward than back, she reasoned. "Indeed, sorrow stalks that house. Perhaps there is something you can do. Perhaps the gods have sent this situation to test you again. Who knows what lies ahead? We can only go one step at a time, and I am tired and hungry."

Hiʻiaka laughed. "Then let us go. Will you rest first or eat?"

"Both at the same time," Wahine-ʻōmaʻo said.

The three women walked along the beach where green waves sighed and splashed into the blue-flowered pōhuehue vines on the dunes. Kalukalu grass waved seed-filled stalks while hala trees slowed their dance as the brisk trade wind changed to the gentle evening breeze.

When they arrived at the little house they heard the sound of chanting inside the house, the chanting of a kahuna lapaʻau, Hiʻiaka realized, a kahuna lapaʻau who really did not know what he was doing. His chant was wrong; he was calling on the wrong gods.

The man by the smoking fire had not seen them coming. Wahine-ʻōmaʻo saw at once that he was trying to heat some stones. They were the wrong size, she noted, for what he was trying to do. Moreover, he did not wait until the rocks glowed red before he snatched one from the fire with two sticks and dropped it into a wooden calabash beside him. A moment later he would remove the rock from the bowl and drop it back into the fire where it would hiss as steam rose to dampen the fire. Then he would blow on the embers, trying to coax a flame back to life and the process would begin again. All the time, he was glancing into the house, his head cocked for better hearing.

Hiʻiaka asked, "What are you doing?"

The man spun around, eyes wide with fright, eyes filled with tears. He crouched over the fire again. "I am cooking lūʻau leaves. My wife wants some."

"Don't you know how to cook lūʻau leaves?" Wahine-ʻōmaʻo asked scornfully. "This is a mess." She looked into the bowl where the latest stone had merely withered the leaves without generating enough heat to cook. The man had not put enough water in the calabash so the leaves were not boiling but being charred by the heat.

"What is wrong with your wife?" Pāʻū-o-palaʻe asked the man. "And what is your name?"

"I am Kalalea," he replied. "My wife is Koʻana-wai. She is sick. The kahuna lapaʻau says she has angered one of the gods but I do not see how. She has always followed their way. Perhaps, he says, she has angered someone and that person has called upon a kahuna ʻanāʻanā who is praying her to death. But I do not think so. She has been ill too long. Black magic is swift, is it not?"

"Yes, it is," Pāʻū-o-palaʻe answered.

"Perhaps your kahuna isn't very knowledgeable," Wahine-ʻōmaʻo said.

"Be careful," The words came from the doorway to the house. An old man with long white hair stuck his head out the door. "I am no amateur. I tell you this woman is very sick. Only by offering the proper sacrifices can she recover."

"What must I offer as sacrifice?" Kalalea asked.

The kahuna stroked his chin, considering. "I shall need some lipoa seaweed from the reef of Molo-aʻa," he said, holding out his hand and pulling one finger flat against his palm. "Then some awa root from Wai-paheʻe." Another finger went down. "Some leaves from the hau trees at

Hō-mai-ka-waʻa, a gourd of water from Uluoma, and last, forty kukui blossoms from Kahiki-kolo." The palm of his hand was gone. Only a fist remained which the old man shook in Kalalea's face. "Get them and we shall see what we can do for your wife."

"It will take time," Kalalea said. "Already it is night. I must wait until dawn."

"Will she last the night?" Wahine-ʻōmaʻo demanded.

"Perhaps," the kahuna replied.

"Perhaps?" Wahine-ʻōmaʻo's voice rose questioningly. She brushed past the kahuna and went into the house. In a few minutes she returned and said to Hiʻiaka, "She will not last the night. She needs something nourishing to eat, like those lūʻau leaves Kalalea is trying to cook. It is only a fever that this stupid kahuna has only made worse. This is something you can easily make right."

"You must go," the kahuna shouted. "You are only making trouble." His words and his tone of voice angered Hiʻiaka. She gestured and the kahuna fell silent, although his lips continued to form words there was no sound. He clutched his throat.

"Leave us," Hiʻiaka ordered. "From now on, only when you speak the truth will your voice be heard. The lies shall remain silent. Go!"

The kahuna stumbled away in the darkness, his eyes wide with fright. Only to speak the truth? His mind reeled.

Hiʻiaka wasted no time. She ordered Kalalea to bring several calabashes of fresh water and a handful of salt. She asked Pāʻū-o-palaʻe to bathe Koʻana-wai and make her comfortable. She did not need to suggest to Wahine-ʻōmaʻo to take the calabash of lūʻau and salvage such leaves as would still be edible and put enough water in the bowl to cover them. After Wahine-ʻōmaʻo did this, Hiʻiaka made the fire blaze up far hotter than the few sticks of driftwood Kalalea had collected could have. The rocks glowed red hot, responding to the sister of the goddess of fire. Hiʻiaka picked up two stones and dropped them into the bowl. The water seethed and boiled. Two rocks were enough to cook the leaves. In moments, Wahine-ʻōmaʻo poured off the boiling water and scooped the lūʻau onto a wooden plate.

Hiʻiaka entered the house. Pāʻū-o-palaʻe was sponging Koʻana-wai's forehead with a damp rag of tapa. Hiʻiaka kneeled beside the bed, a heap of mats woven from kalukalu grass. She ran her hand above the woman's body, without touching her, feeling the mana, the spiritual power that flowed weakly within Koʻana-wai. Wahine-ʻōmaʻo looked questioningly at Hiʻiaka who nodded. Then Hiʻiaka began to chant:

"Come, gods, enter, possess and inspire me,
First you, Kāne-kapolei, god of wildwood,
Hiʻiaka calls you,
For she calls for the power to heal.
Pray enter, and heal, and let live
Koʻana-wai, the ailing woman of Ke-ālia.
Give her life!"

When the chant was done, Hiʻiaka turned to Wahine-ʻōmaʻo. "Was the chant good?" she asked. Wahine-ʻōmaʻo replied, "A bit short, but I don't think that matters in this case."

Waihine-ʻōmaʻo gently lifted the woman's head and Hiʻiaka held up the gourd of water to the woman's mouth and let the water drip gently in. Hiʻiaka slowly passed her hand over the woman's body, listening to the body's messages. "She will live," she told Kalalea. "Let her eat all the lūʻau she wants. Then let her sleep. She will be well by morning."

At dawn, as Hiʻiaka and her companions were ready to continue their journey, Kalalea and Koʻana-wai came out of the house and knelt in front of Hiʻiaka. As they began to speak, Hiʻiaka gestured them to silence. "No need for thanks," Hiʻiaka said. "Name your first daughter after me. That will be enough."

Just once at the top of the trail Hiʻiaka looked back. Koʻana-wai and Kalalea stood looking after them, one hand raised in farewell, the other clutching the hand of their beloved. Hiʻiaka smiled at their love and continued to walk toward the man her sister loved.

Ke Mele a Malae-haʻa-koʻa

THE CHANT OF MALAE-HAʻA-KOʻA
Ke Mele a Malae-haʻa-koʻa

THE SUN HAD ALREADY PASSED BEHIND THE CLIFFS and the puffy evening clouds gleamed orange and yellow when Hiʻiaka-i-ka-poli-o-Pele, her friend Wahine-ʻōmaʻo and her companion Pāʻū-o-palaʻe came to the edge of the Wai-niha river. Hiʻiaka-i-ka-poli-o-Pele was tired and discouraged.

"Hāʻena is around this corner," Hiʻiaka said unhappily. "I do not know what I will find."

"Then we must round the corner and see what we shall see," Wahine-ʻōmaʻo briskly replied. "We must find shelter for the night. It has been a long and dangerous voyage to seek this lover of your sister. First, we must cross this river and then we can ask for shelter at that house over there under the cliff."

Forcing Hiʻiaka to rest under a hau tree, Wahine-ʻōmaʻo lost little time finding a canoe and a man to paddle it. Soon the three women were on the west bank, walking toward the cluster of houses behind a high fence of driftwood gathered from the nearby beach. They could hear the uneven thump of a tapa beater echoing from within but they could not see who was beating. The sound faltered from time to time. Wahine-ʻōmaʻo thought she also heard the sound of stifled sobs. Why was the woman crying? Curious, Wahine-ʻōmaʻo poked a hole in the fence and peered into the compound.

"There is an older woman in the hale kuku kapa," she announced. "And she is crying. Now why would that be?"

Hiʻiaka-i-ka-poli-o-Pele could only think with dread of what she would find around the corner. There would be, she knew, the flats of Naue where the hala trees swayed and danced in the fresh winds. And after that came Hāʻena and its mountains, caves and cliffs. And Lohiʻau, the man for whom she had now traveled many months and through many dangers and evil encounters. And what would she find? She did not know. Had he forgotten Pele? Would he come to Kī-lau-ea? What would happen if he refused? What would Pele do in her rage? For she would be angry, Hiʻiaka-i-ka-poli-o-Pele knew, if Lohiʻau did not come, then it would be the messenger who would be harmed. Suddenly all she wanted to do was sleep and forget.

She chanted to the unseen woman to ask for permission to enter. There was no reply but the beater fell silent. Hiʻiaka-i-ka-poli-o-Pele tried again.

"The mountain turns a cold shoulder
Wai-'ale'ale looks coldly down on Wai-lua.
It is time to bundle up your tapa
To keep it dry during the rains of Ka-wai-kini.
Your lips stay closed.
We go on."

The woman within the fence had not heard Hi'iaka's calls. She was sunk deep in her own sorrow. She was thinking of her husband Malae-ha'a-ko'a, once a proud warrior, now unable to walk, his legs withered and useless. Each morning she carried him to the nearby point where he could cast his fishing line into the ocean and each evening she carried him home again. It hurt her to see him so weak, although he never complained. Tears spilled down her face and, as Hi'iaka-i-ka-poli-o-Pele and Waihine-'ōma'o continued on their way to seek shelter for the night, picked up her beater again. She did not know that Hi'iaka took her silence as proof of haughty and inhospitable conduct.

The sound of the beater echoed the woman's sadness. Wahine-'ōma'o listened and understood. She tugged at Hi'iaka's elbow. "I don't think she heard us," Wahine-'ōma'o said. "Go back and try again."

Hi'iaka shook her head. There was no turning back on this journey.

The path they followed clung to a low cliff at the sea's edge, where one misstep would send them falling onto black wave-washed rocks. As they picked their way, they heard chanting in front of them. Hi'iaka-i-ka-poli-o-Pele, peering ahead, saw a man sitting, his back against a tree, fishing line in hand. He baited his triple-hooked line and leaning toward the waves, spat out freshly chewed fragments of shrimp to attract fish. As he waited he chanted a song.

"The wind pushes the canoe
And blows spray against the cliffs,
Which frightens the fish.
Let there be gentle waves
Here at Wai-niha at the edge of Lulu'upali
To bring food to the fish.

Come, fish, come to my hooks,
The hooks of Malae-haʻa-koʻa."

Hiʻiaka-i-ka-poli-o-Pele's anger against the unseen woman died away, for she realized that this man, whose torso was that of a warrior and whose legs were too weak to support him, was why she wept. Hiʻiaka-i-ka-poli-o-Pele, too, felt sorrow and, in her turn, chanted.

"Malae-haʻa-koʻa, fisherman of the cliffs,
I ask the gods to send you fish,
Fish for the hooks of Malae-haʻa-koʻa."

Such was her power that the wind sank to a whisper, the surface of the sea became calm and a school of akule flocked to Malae-haʻa-koʻa's hooks. He pulled his line out and unhooked three fish, tossed in his line and within moments, pulled out three more.

Malae-haʻa-koʻa looked up from his work, his eye caught by a movement on the path. He did not recognize Hiʻiaka-i-ka-poli-o-Pele but he guessed that it was she who had quieted the wind and the sea. As he gazed at her, he saw the resemblance to the woman who had come to Hāʻena and driven Lohiʻau to his death. At once he knew who that woman was and who this one was, Pele-honua-mea and Hiʻiaka-i-ka-poli-o-Pele.

"It was you then who has made this a day of calm," he said. "I thank you."

"There is no need for thanks," she replied.

He turned back to the sea and threw his fishing line out. "Swarm, fish," he prayed, "swarm to the fisherman's hooks, fish to feed the godlike woman of Puna."

Then he turned back to Hiʻiaka-i-ka-poli-o-Pele when his calabash was filled with akule. "You must return to my home, where even now I heard the faltering sounds of my wife's tapa beater. There you will rest and there you will eat your fill." He picked up his conch shell trumpet. "I shall call for help to carry me home."

Wahine-ʻōmaʻo nudged Hiʻiaka-i-ka-poli-o-Pele. "An opportunity for you," she whispered. "Is your strength enough to heal this small affliction? A test, perhaps, for something harder yet to come. We are not safely home at Pele's door."

"What would you have me do?" Hiʻiaka-i-ka-poli-o-Pele answered.

Wahine-ʻōmaʻo looked at her indignantly. "Surely you do not need me to tell you that," she said.

Hiʻiaka looked at Pāʻū-o-palaʻe waiting patiently. Pāʻū-o-palaʻe put down her bundles, sat on them, and nodded approvingly.

Hiʻiaka-i-ka-poli-o-Pele closed her eyes, composing her thoughts. Then she prayed to the supreme gods, to the goddesses of health and wisdom, and to the four thousand lesser gods. Give her, she prayed, the spiritual power needed to restore the fisherman's legs, to allow him, once again, to walk, to stride, to move without thought. She stopped and looked at Wahine-ʻōmaʻo for her approval.

"It's short," Wahine-ʻōmaʻo said. "You want him to do more than crawl."

Then Hiʻiaka-i-ka-poli-o-Pele prayed again and this time Wahine-ʻōmaʻo nodded approvingly and gestured toward the fisherman. "Look," she said.

Malae-haʻa-koʻa felt a strange tingling throughout his body and he felt youthful strength flooding into his legs, which straightened, and he found himself able to stand on his feet and walk. He knew who had done this for him and he opened wide his arms and held Hiʻiaka-i-ka-poli-o-Pele to him. Then he gathered up his fishing gear, hooks and lines thrust into one basket, fish into another. Taking the two women in the crooks of his elbows, he led them to his home, the same home where they had heard the weeping woman.

When he reached the driftwood fence, he began to tear it down. His wife came rushing out. "What are you doing?" she demanded. "Why are you tearing down our fence?"

And then she realized that he was on his feet, he was moving about as he had as a young warrior and she exclaimed, "What has happened to you? Why are you walking?"

Malae-haʻa-koʻa embraced his wife Ka-noe-lehua and said, "Hiʻiaka-i-ka-poli-o-Pele has cured me," he told her. "We must give them thanks. Call our neighbors and we shall put on a feast Hiʻiaka will never forget."

Wahine-ʻōmaʻo followed Ka-noe-lehua and helped her and her nearby neighbors prepare bundles of sun-dried fish and lūʻau leaves, grated coconuts and fresh taro to make kūlolo, and many other relishes. Meanwhile Malae-haʻa-koʻa with his own hands set about preparing a dog for the oven. For the rest, he sent commands to all the people of Wai-niha to bring whatever was necessary for a feast.

Hiʻiaka-i-ka-poli-o-Pele's offer to help was refused, gently but firmly. "You have cured my husband," said Ka-noe-lehua, "and it is our pleasure to offer thanks to you. Rest, rest. Soon all will be ready. Perhaps you would prefer a swim in the river. We will send someone to show you the way." Ka-noe-lehua sent her three guests to refresh themselves in cold Wai-niha pools. She sent fresh clothing for each of her guests and ordered wreaths of flowers and fern to adorn them.

In the early hours of the night, the feast was ready and everyone fell to with great appetite. When at last all stomachs were full, Malae-ha'a-ko'a and Ka-noe-lehua stood up to sing and dance a song in which they related to the assembly the family connections of the woman who had cured him and in whose honor they were gathered.

He told how Pele, red-haired and fiery, had fought with her sister Nā-maka-o-Kaha'i in far off Kahiki. He told of her flight to the islands of Hawai'i, as swift as the eye-shot of dawn or the flash of lightning. "Elieli kau mai," he prayed at the end of each stanza, "wonder and awe possess me." Hi'iaka-i-ka-poli-o-Pele felt the forces of mana, spiritual power, building within her as Malae-ha'a-ko'a invoked the listening gods.

Then Malae-ha'a-ko'a went on to describe how the ocean waves brought Pele to Hale-ma'uma'u at Kī-lau-ea where she found a home in the midst of an earthquake, during a storm of thunder and pelting rain. Pele came at twilight, tossing and turning on the long-backed waves for the ocean was agitated with jealousy of Pele. The beating of the drum and of the bamboo pipes set the rhythm for Malae-ha'a-ko'a and Ka-noe-lehua as they danced, enacting the surging waves and defiant Pele. "Elieli kau mai," Malae-ha'a-ko'a prayed.

Hi'iaka-i-ka-poli-o-Pele's concentration was broken when Wahine-'ōma'o, sitting next to her, noisily chewed on a tender morsel of bone with a great smacking of the lips. "Hush!" Hi'iaka-i-ka-poli-o-Pele said. "Observe the dignity of this occasion by eating more quietly."

Wahine-'ōma'o, always one to put the important things first, finished the food in front of her for she felt that she would insult her hosts by not showing proper appreciation for their food. Indeed, the feast was worth a loud smacking of the lips. She ate quietly and only then turned her attention to the song and dancers before her.

"For whom do I make this offering of song?" chanted Malae-ha'a-ko'a. "Pele is my god. Elieli kau mai!"

At his acceptance of Pele as a god, Hi'iaka-i-ka-poli-o-Pele felt the mana within surge into full force, renewing her, giving her strength for what came next in her search for her sister's husband, for Lohi'au, handsome chief of Hā'ena.

The dancing continued long into the night and it was very late in the morning before anyone rose. The sun was overhead when Malae-haʻa-koʻa and Ka-noe-lehua joined Hiʻiaka-i-ka-poli-o-Pele at the ocean side.

"You have come a long way," Malae-haʻa-koʻa said. "What is the purpose of your visit?"

"I have come to bring chief Lohiʻau to my sister as husband," Hiʻiaka-i-ka-poli-o-Pele replied.

"Lohiʻau has been dead for many days," Ka-noe-lehua said. "He took his own life because of his love for a woman."

"And that woman was Pele," Malae-haʻa-koʻa said. "I see that now. That is why you have come. But it is a long voyage for nothing."

"Let that be as it may," Hiʻiaka-i-ka-poli-o-Pele said. "Thanks to you, my strength is renewed. I will go on to Hāʻena and see for myself."

"You will always have a home here," Malae-haʻa-koʻa said. "Always."

Hiʻiaka-i-ka-poli-o-Pele smiled. "I shall remember that." Then she turned to her friends and companions. "Wahine-ʻōmaʻo, Pāʻū-o-palaʻe, it is time to go."

Wahine-ʻōmaʻo protested. It is late, she pointed out, where would they spend the night? What about food? Madness to go at dusk. But Pāʻū-o-palaʻe simply bundled up their few possessions and stood waiting. Accepting the use of a guide, Hiʻiaka-i-ka-poli-o-Pele embraced Malae-haʻa-koʻa and Ka-noe-lehua and started for Hāʻena and Lohiʻau.

Ka Hewa a Pākamoi

CHRISTINE FAYÉ·01

THE MISTAKE OF PĀKAMOI
Ka Hewa a Pākamoi

THE JOURNEY WAS ALMOST OVER. It had been a long time since she and Hiʻiaka had set out from Hale-maʻumaʻu to go to Kauaʻi and bring back Lohiʻau to Pele. Pāʻū-o-palaʻe had gladly slung their travel-ing bundles over her shoulder and followed Hiʻiaka. She had thought it would be a matter of a walk to Hilo, a canoe ride to Kauaʻi and back, and then a last walk through the forest of ʻōhiʻa lehua trees Hiʻiaka loved so much.

Pāʻū-o-palaʻe sighed. It had not been that simple. There were evil moʻo along the way, each determined to destroy Hiʻiaka, and there had been battles to clear the way. There had been enemies who had not wanted Pele to take Lohiʻau as a husband and tried to hinder Hiʻiaka but these, too, had been overcome. The only good thing, Pāʻū-o-palaʻe thought, was that they had met Wahine-ʻōmaʻo and she came with them and had become a friend.

The journey had taught Pāʻū-o-palaʻe that nothing really was as it first appeared. A pleasant face hid an ugly spirit. The simplest river crossing could turn into a clash of wills, turn into a life or death situation without her really understanding why or how.

Hiʻiaka, Wahine-ʻōmaʻo and Pāʻū-o-palaʻe left the cliff of Luluʻupali and walked across the sandy plains of Naue following their guide, Pākamoi, who they had been told, was a lawaiʻa kīhele-hele ʻulua, an expert fisherman of the ulua traveling here and there in schools. What that had to do with his knowing the way to Hāʻena and Lohiʻau, Pāʻū-o-palaʻe did not know. She eyed him suspi-ciously for outer appearances gave no sure clue to future events.

Pākamoi was neither young nor old, his hair was still black, his muscular body just starting to sag with age. He thought himself good looking, one could see that, Pāʻū-o-palaʻe thought, in the way he preened, the way he leaned toward Hiʻiaka, almost caressing her as they walked. Hiʻiaka was pay-ing no attention. She was looking into the hills on their left, looking toward the mountain slope where Pekeu waterfall slid and tumbled sideways instead of straight down. Wahine-ʻōmaʻo plodded ahead, as she always did, keeping her eye on Hiʻiaka and guiding her by the elbow from time to time to bring her back onto the path.

Pākamoi was happy. He was in the company of three beautiful women. There was Pāʻū-o-palaʻe, slender, fair of face. There was Wahine-ʻōmaʻo, sturdy, lines of laughter lining her eyes and mouth. There was Hiʻiaka, tall, regal, beautiful, reddish hair. Surely he could win one of them this night.

"Not long now," he said. "Makana is visible now. The hālau hula lies just beyond that and Ka-hua-nui will offer you her hospitality."

"We don't want to spend the night with people," Wahine-'ōma'o said. "We will sleep where no one will bother us."

Pākamoi's chest leaped. Did he understand her correctly? "There is the upper wet cave," he said. "There is a grove of trees at the opening that will give us shelter."

"That will do, perhaps," said Wahine-'ōma'o.

The sun was sinking and the sky was clear. It would be a good evening to spend out-of-doors, although Pā'ū-o-pala'e would much have preferred the hospitality of the hālau hula.

The sun was gone by the time they reached the cave. They wound about large rocks and into a grove of kukui trees. They came to a jumble of sheltered rocks with enough room between one boulder and another to build up a bed to sleep on, which would be protected on two sides by stone under a canopy of a kukui tree.

Hi'iaka drew in her breath sharply. She was looking along the face of the cliff that loomed above them. She pointed and whispered to Wahine-'ōma'o, "Do you see that?"

"See what?" Wahine-'ōma'o returned sharply. "It's almost too dark to see anything."

"I thought I saw a wailua, the spirit of a person flitting along the cliff. There is a cave there. Perhaps someone has died and is buried there and its soul has not yet found its way to the realm of Milu."

"Perhaps," said Wahine-'ōma'o. "Perhaps not. It may be a dragonfly. We shall see better in the morning."

"There are plenty of ferns." Pākamoi said. We can pick them and make a comfortable bed for ourselves."

Pā'ū-o-pala'e recognized the game Pākamoi was playing. Hi'iaka, she knew, did not. Hi'iaka was not paying attention to this fisherman who thought he had three ulua within moments of being caught.

Pā'ū-o-pala'e put down her bundles. "We need fern and leaves," she told Pākamoi. They began to gather them and Pā'ū-o-pala'e piled them between the boulders and against the trunk of the kukui until a deep bed had been made, a comfortable hikie'e for them to sleep on.

When that was done, Pākamoi lit a small fire, and roasted a yam over it. While it was cooking, Pākamoi tried to engage Hi'iaka in conversation. She barely listened but that only inspired him to try his hand at composing a chant on the spot. He sang of ferns and of the Milky Way, now shining clearly above them. He referred to the ferns he had picked for their bed and as all four would be sleeping under the Milky Way, so, too, could the four of them sleep together under the ferns.

"Yes, yes," Hiʻiaka said impatiently, for his words were no more than the buzzing of a nalo, a fly, making too much noise and calling unwelcome attention to itself. "Let us eat."

Pākamoi took the yam from the fire and sliced it into thin lengthwise pieces, which resembled the snout of a lizard. They ate and then Hiʻiaka rose. "It is time to sleep," she said.

Pākamoi remained at the fire and watched the three woman go to their bed of fern. He watched as they loosened their skirts so that they could sleep more comfortably. First Wahine-ʻōmaʻo fell asleep and her breath came in deep rumbles, almost a snore. Then Pāʻū-o-palaʻe stretched on her side and closed her eyes and her chest rose and fell in the steady rhythm that means sleep.

Only Hiʻiaka tossed, rolling from this side to that. Then he heard her call, saw her hand gesturing as though greeting someone, and Pākamoi jumped to his feet and went to join Hiʻiaka in her bed.

When he kneeled beside Hiʻiaka, reaching to pull her skirt to one side, Pāʻū-o-palaʻe rose to her knees and threw herself into his arms.

"At last you have come," she cried loudly.

"Hush," whispered Pākamoi, "you'll wake them."

"They are too tired, they will sleep," she shouted. "Come, come over here."

As she moved backwards, she jabbed her foot into Wahine-ʻōmaʻo's side. Wahine-ʻōmaʻo awoke at once. She saw Pāʻū-o-palaʻe struggling in Pākamoi's embrace; it was hard to tell whether he was forcing himself on her or trying to get away. She reached out and touched Hiʻiaka's shoulder. When Hiʻiaka's eyes opened, Wahine-ʻōmaʻo gestured toward the struggling couple.

Hiʻiaka saw what was happening with astonishment. Only when she looked into Pāʻū-o-palaʻe's agonized eyes, did she realize what was happening and why. She was furious.

"Get away!" she ordered the fisherman. "Leave her!"

Pāʻū-o-palaʻe let him go and he stumbled to his feet and moved backwards. Hiʻiaka let him take a few more steps, then she fixed her blazing eyes on him.

Pākamoi stared into her eyes. He could not look away. He felt his feet turn numb, then his knees, followed by his belly and chest. He glanced down once and saw that he was turning to stone and looked up again, fear carved into his face and opened his mouth to plead with Hiʻiaka, too late. He had made a terrible mistake. In a moment he had turned to stone, all that remained of Pākamoi, the fisherman.

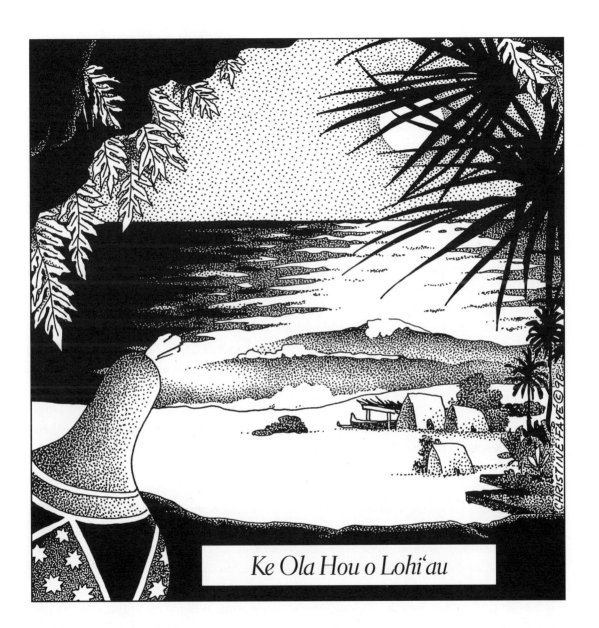

Ke Ola Hou o Lohiʻau

LOHI'AU IS RESTORED TO LIFE
Ke Ola Hou o Lohi'au

KA-HUA-NUI LEANED AGAINST THE STONE WALL that held her brother's house, now a tomb for his body until such time as his bones would be wrapped and hidden for safe keeping for all time. She remembered bitterly the night when the strange fiery-haired woman had appeared at the hālau hula entrance and had so bewitched her brother Lohi'au that after three days and three nights, he had hanged himself in despair when she left him. Better if she had never come, Ka-hua-nui thought.

Now there was only silence. There were no sounds of drums, no hollow gourd instruments beat to set the rhythm of the dance, voices of no musical instruments echoed from the cliffs. Kilioe, the head of the hula school, had disappeared. For weeks Kilioe had been distracted, lost in some reverie of her own and unaware of those around her. Ever since, Ka-hua-nui thought, those strange half-flowered plants had been discovered, one at the beach of Lumaha'i, the other far up the ridge towards Wai-'ale'ale. With Kilioe gone, there was no one in charge. Ka-hua-nui knew she should take the leadership; she had been trained for it. But she could not organize herself well enough to issue orders and so the students wandered aimlessly, at first chanting or practicing their steps but now, after several days, they spent their days idling in the shade of the milo trees practicing the dances and songs they already knew.

The leader of the school of history, Ka-lei-paoa, had left to offer special prayers on Ni'ihau for the rest and repose of Lohi'au's spirit. He had taken his pupils with him. Now, where there had been the sound of chants, the murmuring sounds of names repeated over and over until they could not escape the memory, these were gone.

Ka-hua-nui remembered her childhood when she had two brothers to play with and command and tease, Lohi'au and Lima-loa. Now Lima-loa had disappeared, rumors said he had gone to join the woman of the Mānā mirage. If so, it had only just happened, for he had come to Hā'ena when he heard his brother was dead, had helped lay out his body and thatched the pili grass roof. And Lohi'au was dead. Ka-hua-nui felt beaten down by grief. Deep in her own thoughts, she did not see the three women walking along the path toward her. She did not see when one pointed up at the sheer face of Makana, the mountain of the fiery arrows. When this figure began to chant, Ka-hua-nui was shocked at the intrusion of sound into the dead silence of Hā'ena.

Hiʻiaka-i-ka-poli-o-Pele, for it was she, pointed to something flitting along the face of the cliff. "Do you see that?" she demanded of Wahine-ʻōmaʻo.

"No," said Waihine-ʻōmaʻo. "What is there to see but the shadow of koaʻe birds and clouds?"

"I see what seems to be a ghost at the mouth of a cave," Pāʻū-o-palaʻe said.

Hiʻiaka concentrated her spiritual powers on the dim figure. "Ah," she sighed, "It is Lohiʻau. It is true he has died."

"Then we must return to Pele and tell her so," Wahine-ʻōmaʻo said. She was weary of this trip and wanted to see her home forests of giant tree ferns and lehua trees again.

"She ordered me to bring Lohiʻau to her," Hiʻiaka reminded her. "I will do so."

"But he is dead!" Wahine-ʻōmaʻo said in dismay.

Pāʻū-a-palaʻe said, "Not if you help her restore him to life. You must listen to her prayers and tell her if she goes wrong with them. You must be the judge. Meanwhile I will go and find us a place to sleep and some food for later." Pāʻū-a-palaʻe turned and walked along the banks of taro patches towards a cluster of houses.

Hiʻiaka extended her hand, palm up, in a gesture of welcome and called to the indistinct figure flickering at the cave entrance.

> "Beloved man of the Hāʻena cliffs,
>   The never ending cliffs
>   That stretch from Hoʻolulu to Poli-hale,
>   Beloved man, come back!"

There was no answer, but it seemed to Hiʻiaka that the figure had fixed its attention on her. Surely it was listening!

> "You, surely, are not the lover
>   To cling to in the twilight,
>   To hold in the time of sleep,
>   Beloved man, come back!"

A faint cry came down the cliff to their waiting ears.

> "Beloved woman!
>   You have failed to recognize me.

I have waited for you in the cliffs
between Ka-lalau and Ho‘olulu.
Beloved woman, come back!"

Hi‘iaka realized that the spirit of Lohi‘au thought that his beloved Pele had returned for him. She could feel a stirring in her own heart for this man, pity that his love for Pele had driven him to such despair. She would bring him back to life, she promised herself. We will wander the uplands of Ka-lalau, you and I, she thought, through the wind-driven mist, the kili-hau, and the rain that makes no splash as it falls into the cool mountain waters, the kili-opu. She realized suddenly that he was the man she had dreamed of for herself. For a moment, she stood in sorrow, for she had promised to bring him to her sister without touching him. Promises were sacred and so she would do what she had promised, even though it could break her heart.

"Your voice is the trilling cry
Of the pololei land shell of Ālealea-lau,
Whose song is carried by Lani-ku‘ua,
The night wind of Ka-lalau.
Let us speak together,
Come to me, beloved man of Hā‘ena."

The spirit of Lohi‘au drifted from the cave entrance and floated down closer to Hi‘iaka. When it was the size of a small white moth, Hi‘iaka snatched it within her cupped hands.

"Quickly," she said to Wahine-‘ōma‘o, "get me something to put this spirit into."

"I have nothing!" Wahine-‘ōma‘o protested. "What can I use?"

"Empty out our water gourd," Hi‘iaka ordered. And Wahine-‘ōma‘o uncorked the long-necked gourd and poured the water onto the ground. Carefully Hi‘iaka forced the fluttering moth into the gourd and corked it again. Sighing with relief, Hi‘iaka said, "Now we must find the body." She led the way looking for someone who could answer her questions.

Ka-hua-nui looked up as Hi‘iaka approached her. "I heard your chants," she said, " and it is obvious that you loved my brother, even though you never knew him, my handsome brother, dead! If only he had fallen in love with you instead of that other woman. What a waste, to end his life for the likes of her!"

"And yet she has sent me for him, as she promised," Hi'iaka said. "Do not waste time with recriminations. I have captured his spirit; now I must find his body. Where is it?"

Ka-hua-nui pointed to the stone wall behind her. "On top of this wall is a platform," she said, "and on that platform is Lohi'au's house. Lima-loa himself rethatched it before he and all the others left to offer prayers on Ni'ihau. Only I and my husband remain to stand guard." Ka-hua-nui led Hi'iaka up the path that led to the platform and swept aside the tapa that covered the doorway.

Hi'iaka glanced within. "You have been deceived by Lima-loa. He did not build a house to entomb your brother. He stole the body instead."

"No," Ka-hua-nui protested. "His body is here. That is why I keep guard. No one can disturb his rest."

"Someone has," Hi'iaka said tartly. "Look for yourself."

Ka-hua-nui rushed into the house but there was no body there. She turned, bewildered, to Hi'iaka, who was carefully scanning the cliffs above them. She focused her attention on the cave where she had first seen the cowering spirit. She saw two women squatting at the entrance of the cave, thinking they were unseen. They were, Hi'iaka discovered as her mind probed into theirs, guarding Lohi'au's body. It was they who had stolen it. Hi'iaka called out to them.

"E! Aka and Kilioe,
Experts of the dance,
Why are you hiding above the healing pond
The crystal water of Hala-aniani
Let me join you,
Let me mourn with you.
I seek Lohi'au, the loved one of Hā'ena."

Hi'iaka felt their eyes fix on her, a gaze of defiance and even of hatred. They did not answer Hi'iaka's call.

Hi'iaka said to Ka-hua-nui, "Return to your hula school and keep the joyful sounds of the hula going continuously for the next ten days. I want everyone's attention drawn to you; no one must look upwards and perhaps see me and break my concentration."

"It will be so," Ka-hua-nui said and ran to find her students.

"Now," Hi'iaka said to Wahine-'ōma'o, "we must climb to that cave."

Wahine-ʻōmaʻo was aghast. "There is no ladder for us to climb up on," she said.

"Then turn your face to the cliff," Hiʻiaka ordered, "and start to climb."

Wahine-ʻōmaʻo protested, "The day is late and evening will soon he here. We cannot climb there in the dark; let us wait for tomorrow."

Hiʻiaka glanced at the sun. "Have no fear," she said. "It will not get dark until we wish it so." And Hiʻiaka called to the sun, asking it to stand still as it crossed the Hea stream at the entrance of Hāʻena. She ended her prayer with, "Stand still, O Sun, over Hea stream!" The sun stopped its relentless journey to the west for a time.

The two women clung to the cliff face as though they had the clinging feet of geckos. Slowly they approached the cave entrance where Aka and Kilioe stood.

"Go back," Kilioe called. "Do not come here!"

"You would do better to let us come," Hiʻiaka replied. "Leave the cave and leave Lohiʻau. No harm will come to you."

Kilioe laughed. "You have killed moʻo people during your entire voyage. Now I shall kill you!" Kilioe swung her sling again and again, speeding water-worn pebbles at Hiʻiaka. Wahine-ʻōmaʻo yelled as one struck her leg. If one of these rocks hit either woman on the head, they could fall senseless to the ground below. Hiʻiaka gathered her mana, her spiritual powers, and called upon her gods for help to turn Kilioe and Aka to stone. Aka fell to the ground at the foot of the cliff. Kilioe tried to escape and fled along the cliff towards the safety of the Nāpali valleys but, just above the hālau hula where she once had been leader, she, too, felt herself changing into stone and fell, coming to rest on the edge of the sea.

Hiʻiaka and Wahine-ʻōmaʻo entered the cave. Hiʻiaka knelt beside Lohiʻau's body. He lay on a bed of lauhala mats, He looked like a man who had fallen asleep. There was no sign of decay.

"Light a fire," Hiʻiaka ordered Wahine-ʻōmaʻo.

Wahine-ʻōmaʻo gathered scraps of wood from the cave floor and rubbed fire sticks together. As the fire flared up, the sun continued its journey. As the last glow of a brilliant sunset faded, Wahine-ʻōmaʻo prepared leaves of fragrant medicinal plants. These Hiʻiaka placed on Lohiʻau's body at the seven nerve centers of the body.

"You must hold his feet," said Hiʻiaka to Wahine-ʻōmaʻo. Wahine-ʻōmaʻo grasped his ankles as Hiʻiaka cut a hole in his big toe and, opening the water gourd, forced the reluctant spirit to enter its former body.

"Now, listen to my prayer," Hiʻiaka said. "If it is correct and well said and there are no interruptions, Lohiʻau will live. Otherwise he will die."

"He will not survive," Wahine-ʻōmaʻo said gloomily.

Hiʻiaka began her prayer. First she called upon the female gods. She prayed to Hānai-a-ka-mālama, the goddess who gave a chief the taboos that were his birthright. She called on Mai-uʻu and Ma-aʻa, goddesses of the wilderness who strung wreaths to decorate the superior gods, and to Nahinahi-ana, the goddess who made the dyes used in coloring and printing tapa. She then prayed to the god Kū, especially Kū-hulu who had charge of life-giving water, as well as the god Kāne, god of all living things, and to all his family. She finished with "He waimaka, he waimaka aloha, I weep, I weep with love. Let my prayer speed on its way!"

Wahine-ʻōmaʻo could feel that Lohiʻau's spirit had advanced as far as his knees. The spirit faltered and wanted to turn back but Wahine-ʻōmaʻo blocked its way with her hands.

"What do you think of my prayer?" Hiʻiaka asked

"It was a good prayer," Wahine-ʻōmaʻo said. "Its only fault is that it was over too quickly. The spirit got only to the knees before the prayer was over."

"I shall pray again. If it is a good prayer, Lohiʻau will live."

"And if it is a bad prayer, Lohiʻau will die," Wahine-ʻōmaʻo replied. "I am listening."

In her second prayer, Hiʻiaka prayed to her brother Ka-moho-aliʻi, asking that he bring all their comrades from the burning pit, those who would befriend Lohiʻau. She prayed to Kū and his family, to Ku-wala, the god that presided at the hauling of a canoe log, to Ku-haili-moe, who brought the dreams at night; to the gods that presided over the kukui oil lamps. Then she prayed to another brother, Lono-makua, who was the guardian of fire and of life-force. "Come!" she pleaded. "Answer my prayers and bring Lohiʻau to life."

Wahine-ʻōmaʻo saw that the spirit had reached the heart for blood was flowing through the body. As yet the spirit had not reclaimed the head and life was not yet completely restored to Lohiʻau.

"What do you think of my prayer?" Hiʻiaka asked. She knew that success or failure depended upon the quality of her prayer, the way she said it, to the prayer being free to go on its way to the gods without noise or a disturbance of any kind. Hiʻiaka, while she was praying, was unaware of the world around her. Had an ʻalae called? A dog barked? Had she forgotten a god or goddess? Had her words been clearly spoken so that the listening gods would not mistake their names? All these she needed to know, and no one was better to tell her the truth than Wahine-ʻōmaʻo.

"So far," Wahine-ʻōmaʻo said, "your prayers are good enough for most purposes. But they are too short here. Lohiʻau's spirit has only reached his heart; life has not yet returned. Try again."

Hiʻiaka sprinkled the body with water and began to pray again. On and on it went, for the spirit rebelled as it came to the neck and turned back. Wahine-ʻōmaʻo put fresh aromatic leaves and massaged Lohiʻau's legs and arms, always seeking to catch the spirit and force it a little farther. Not until it reached the eyes and peered out into the world would the process of restoring life be completed. Hour after hour, the prayer of Hiʻiaka echoed within the cave; hour after hour Wahine-ʻōmaʻo massaged and coaxed the spirit further and further up, and the two women could feel the air around them vibrate with the presence of the gods Hiʻiaka had invoked and asked for help. It was like the build up of a charge of lightning and the effect on the two women was like the effect of a lightning flash as Lohiʻau gave a crowing sigh as his chest rose and air rushed into his lungs. He opened his eyes and looked about him in complete bewilderment.

He found himself in a small rocky cave with two women kneeling beside him, women he'd never seen before. He looked out of the cave's opening and saw the taro fields below him, the sand dunes, and the breakers rolling in towards the reef, breakers such as he had often surfed on his board. A great longing to surf filled him.

"How are you, Lohiʻau?" Hiʻiaka asked.

"I am well," he said, sitting up and looking curiously at him.

"I have come from Pele," Hiʻiaka said, "and I will take you to her." She saw his flinch as he recalled who Pele was and what he had done in despair. "But I have been a long time on my journey and have little time to fulfill my promise to Pele. We must leave now."

"No," Lohiʻau replied, "not before I have surfed once again will I leave." He stood and Hiʻiaka could see why Pele had fallen in love with him. He was tall and there were no blemishes anywhere on him. "Let us surf together," he said to Hiʻiaka. Hiʻiaka refused him with a shake of her head.

Wahine-ʻōmaʻo asked, "How are we going to get down from here? I'm not like a lizard that can climb face down a cliff."

Hiʻiaka gestured and three rainbows appeared at the entrance to the cave and arched down to the beach. Hiʻiaka grasped both Lohiʻau and Wahine-ʻōmaʻo with her hands and, pulling them with her, raced down the arches, stepping on the sand as a breaker foamed at their feet, bringing a long surfboard to Lohiʻau's feet.

With a shout of joy, he fell on the board and paddled out into the surf where he caught wave after wave as the moon lit his path through the phosphorescent waves.

Hiʻiaka watched him but Wahine-ʻōmaʻo was soon bored. She saw a woman walking down the beach toward them. She nudged Hiʻiaka. "Here comes a woman," she said.

"His sister, Ka-hua-nui," Hiʻiaka said.

Wahine-ʻōmaʻo called to her by name and went to greet her.

"The noise of the hula drums has given me a headache. They have not stopped for ten days and ten nights. I came to listen to the booming of the waves. Whenever they sound like this, I remember that Lohiʻau delighted in surfing. I came to remember him."

"Where is your husband?" Wahine-ʻōmaʻo asked.

"At home and asleep," Ka-hua-nui replied.

"Wake him and tell him to go over to Niʻihau and bring everybody back. Look, Lohiʻau is alive and well. That is he with the surfboard out there."

Ka-hua-nui stared for a moment then turned and ran back to her house, shouting for her husband, Ke-koa-ola. She told him the wonderful news and he shoved his canoe down the slope of the beach, checked the outrigger lashings, put paddles and bailers in their proper places, stepped the mast, raised the sails and launched the canoe on its journey to Niʻihau. Within hours, Paoa hurried ashore to greet his friend Lohiʻau once more. Lohiʻau, quiet and subdued, was sitting with his sister and two strange women.

Lohiʻau gestured toward the two strange women. "Greet these two who have brought me to life again."

"Where are they from?" Paoa asked, round-eyed with wonder.

"I do not know," Lohiʻau replied, "for I have not had a time to ask. I only know they have given me life."

Ka-hua-nui said, warmly embracing first Hiʻiaka and then Wahine-ʻōmaʻo, "It was worthwhile for my brother to have died to find two such beautiful women as you."

"The other one is more beautiful than we are," Hiʻiaka said, "as Lohiʻau knows."

"And where is this other woman?" Ka-hua-nui asked, filled with foreboding.

"Toward the sunrise," Hiʻiaka said. "And I must bring Lohiʻau to her."

"What is the name of the island on which this woman lives?" Ka-hua-nui asked.

"Hawaiʻi," came the answer.

"And the woman is..."

"Pele-honua-mea." Paoa said the name. "The goddess of the volcanic fires. It was she who lured you to your death."

"And I must go to her," Lohi'au said.

Later that day, Ke-koa-ola again prepared his canoe but this time headed for the island of Hawai'i, bringing with him Hi'iaka and Lohi'au, the beloved of Pele-honua-mea.

Ke Kaʻao a Wahine-ʻōmaʻo

Wahine-'Ōma'o's Story
Ke Ka'ao a Wahine-'ōma'o

Wahine-'ōma'o was afraid. She was nearing home again, within the forests of lehua trees and 'ama'u fern that stretched from the sea at Hilo to the home of Pele-honua-mea at Kī-lau-ea. This was familiar land. She knew where she was and which path to follow to reach her childhood home. This was the end of the journey. She should be filled with relief that the journey was over, but she was afraid.

She had joined Hi'iaka-i-ka-poli-o-Pele in this same forest at the beginning of her mission to find the man Pele had chosen as husband for herself. Wahine-'ōma'o had followed Hi'iaka ever since, through battle after battle with the forces of the mo'o, lizard creatures who opposed the power of Pele. She had followed Hi'iaka across the channel to Maui, on to Moloka'i and O'ahu, and on to Kaua'i. They had reached Hā'ena to find that Lohi'au, the sweetheart of Pele, had died. Hi'iaka had seen his soul fluttering helplessly against the cliffs, caught it and restored it to his body. Now here they were, at the end of their journey.

"Go," Pele had said, "bring Lohi'au to me. Within forty days bring him to me."

But the errand had taken far longer than that. Pele was like fire, warm and loving at times, ferocious and life-devouring at others. Her temper was also like fire, dying down into faint embers, then flaring up like a fountain of lava. At best, Pele's temper was unpredictable. Wahine-'ōma'o worried. If she were truly angry, what would she do?

Hi'iaka tossed a wreath of palapalai fern and lehua blossoms she had woven to Wahine-'ōma'o. "Wear this for me," she said. As they walked along, Hi'iaka picked more fern and lehua, ignoring the misty rain gently wetting them.

Wahine-'ōma'o followed behind Hi'iaka and Lohi'au. They had fallen silent now. On the journey from Kaua'i, they had laughed and created new chants to amuse themselves. Slowly their eyes had met more often, their hands had lingered just a little longer, and Wahine-'ōma'o had noted each change. Lohi'au little by little had begun to forget the woman who had so enchanted him. There was an attraction between Hi'iaka and Lohi'au, like the build-up of a charge of lightning from a storm approaching shore. Only Hi'iaka's promise to her sister kept her away from Lohi'au's arms; this and Pele's promise to protect Hi'iaka's lehua forest and her friend Hōpoe who lived there. As long as Hi'iaka remained aloof, Pele would not care, for Pele intended Lohiʻau to be her husband for only a few days before she would gladly give him away to who-ever wanted him.

So Wahine-ʻōmaʻo was not surprised to see a shimmering sheet of hardened pāhoehoe spreading down the slopes of Mauna Loa to the sea, covering Hiʻiaka's lehua grove, home of her friend Hōpoe. Pele had broken her promise.

Wahine-ʻōmaʻo saw the changing looks cross Hiʻiaka's face. First the disbelief, then the sorrow. She wailed, and called upon all the gods to look upon her sorrow and at the deadly result of Pele's broken promise. Her voice echoed within the caldera in front of her. The world grew silent, listening to her sorrow. Hiʻiaka's sisters and her two brothers came to the entrance of their home. Even Pele herself came to look, drawn by the power of Hiʻiaka's cry of sorrow.

Wahine-ʻōmaʻo tried to hold Hiʻiaka back but Hiʻiaka shrugged off her hand and turned to Lohiʻau. She placed a lei of lehua flowers around his neck and, holding him by the shoulders, pressed her nose against his, a kiss whose meaning no one could fail to recognize, the kiss of a woman claiming at long last the man she loves.

Pele snarled. She raised her hand and lava began to bubble up within the caldera, a fiery hot fountain began, first a little trickle that quickly blossomed into a huge fountain that rose high into the sky. Hot cinders began to fall on the embracing couple. Hiʻiaka broke away from Lohiʻau's arms.

"This is Pele's embrace, these cinders," she said to Lohiʻau. "This is her greeting to you. You must go."

"I will not leave you," Lohiʻau said.

"She will kill you," Hiʻiaka told him.

"She has already done so once," he replied. "If she chooses to kill me again, I can do nothing. But I will not leave you, now that I have found you."

"I am your death," Hiʻiaka mourned. "All I love Pele will destroy with her jealousy and anger."

The cinders fell, a hot rain that began to pile deeper and deeper around the bodies of the three standing on the edge of the caldera. Lohiʻau, no longer protected by Pele's love, knew that in a short time the cinders would cover him. He looked into Hiʻiaka's eyes for he knew that would be the last thing he would see and what he would remember in Pō where his spirit would go. With his last breath, he sang one last song to his beloved.

"Farewell! We became friends
As we traveled the road to Hale-ma'uma'u.
Now death overturns life once again.
I have no gift, no offering to give you,
Only this chanted prayer.
Hi'iaka-i-ka-poli-o-Pele,
To you! To you! Aloha!"

He was almost covered now. Hi'iaka's tears flowed down her cheeks as she replied.

"Farewell, my companion of the misty rain
That sprinkled the lehua trees as we rested at noon
And wove wreaths in the rain that gives flowers life.
My lehua forest has been burned to embers,
Gone are those I love, Hōpoe and Lohi'au.
You are a warrior of wind against Pele-honua-mea.
I brought you to your death here at Pu'u-lena.
Your fate is the long sleep, death.
Farewell, Lohi'au, my love from Hā'ena.
Lohi'au, my love is yours."

The cinders covered Lohi'au and hardened into stone. Lohi'au was gone. Hi'iaka wailed again, the sorrowful wail over the body of a loved one. Then she ran down the slopes to the sea where her forest had stood. "Two times you have destroyed those I love," Hi'iaka said with deep anger, "never again, Pele, never again!"

Hi'iaka began to dig a hole into the earth, leaving a thin shell to keep the ocean from entering until she was ready for it. She dug intently through the first of the ten walls Pele had placed between her and the surging waves. She broke through the second wall.

Pele's brother Ka-moho-ali'i asked Wahine-'ōma'o, "What is Hi'iaka doing?"

Wahine-'ōma'o snorted scornfully. "Can't you see?" she asked. "She is digging a tunnel."

Hi'iaka continued digging and passed through the third wall. Seven more to go and she would be face to face with Pele. The fourth wall was breached.

Pele's brothers grew nervous. Kū-moku-aliʻi asked, "Why is she digging a tunnel?"

"At one end, the fire-killing sea," Wahine-ʻōmaʻo answered. "At the other, Pele sits warming herself with her fire. For how long? What will happen with water meets fire?"

"She will do this?" Ka-moho-aliʻi said in alarm. "She will destroy the world?"

"A promise is a sacred thing," Wahine-ʻōmaʻo replied. "Pele broke her word."

Hiʻiaka continued through the fifth and sixth walls.

"You must stop Hiʻiaka," Kū-moku-aliʻi said.

"I?" snorted Wahine-ʻōmaʻo. "You are gods not I."

"We cannot stop her," Ka-moho-aliʻi said. "Already our strength weakens."

"Pele feels the danger," Kū-moku-aliʻi. "Our place is with her. Come, brother, we must go."

"Only you can save us all," Ka-moho-aliʻi told Wahine-ʻōmaʻo. "Only you." The brothers faded away and were gone.

Wahine-ʻōmaʻo pondered the situation. Hiʻiaka was digging a tunnel, which would reach from the sea to the firepit. Once that was done, Hiʻiaka would let the sea in and the water would drown Pele's fire and the earth itself would change, perhaps even be destroyed along with every human and bird and plant, all living things would be gone. Even Hiʻiaka herself. Love for Hiʻiaka filled Wahine-ʻōmaʻo. She deserved to live and to love.

Wahine-ʻōmaʻo set her kino wailua, her spiritual form, free and sent it flying to Kauaʻi, to Hāʻena, home of Lohiʻau and of his friend, Ka-lei-paoa. He was standing at the altar of his heiau.

"Come and say farewell to your friend," Wahine-ʻōmaʻo told him. "He is at Kī-lau-ea."

Ka-lei-paoa turned to her. "Lohiʻau is in trouble?"

"He is dead," she said and told him of the cold fury of Hiʻiaka.

Ka-lei-paoa replied, "It is that woman's fault. I shall find her and pull out her eyelashes and fill her mouth with dirt."

Wahine-ʻōmaʻo thought he was being foolish, for obviously he did not knew Pele's power. She was a goddess, he a human. No matter, she thought, I need him on Hawaiʻi. "Come to Hawaiʻi quickly," the kino wailua of Wahine-ʻōmaʻo said, and faded away.

Hiʻiaka was digging her way through the ninth wall. Soon she would uncover the fires of Pele. Wahine-ʻōmaʻo called out to her.

> "It is night at Hāʻena and the ocean spray beckons.
> At Kēʻē a small fire can warm the body.

Night is coming on but it will soon pass,
A friend for you in the misty rain is coming,
A friend to guard you against the mountain cold
And the drizzling chilly rain.
Are you listening? Hear me!
The warm trade wind rains wait for you."

Hi'iaka shook her head, unwilling to listen to her friend's words. She continued digging. Wahine-'ōma'o took hold of her elbow and held it tightly. "Come with me," she said. "Let us return to the sunshine and the breezes and the rain and life."

"I will avenge Lohi'au first," Hi'iaka muttered.

"You will destroy the world for him?" Wahine-'ōma'o said sarcastically. "Oh, well done, indeed. All of us must suffer for a broken promise. What of us? What of the man who awaits you?"

"Lohi'au?" Hi'iaka asked hopefully.

"No," Wahine-'ōma'o replied. "Not Lohi'au. His friend, Ka-lei-paoa."

"I do not know him," Hi'iaka said.

"You will," Wahine-'ōma'o said.

Hi'iaka began to weep and Wahine-'ōma'o led her back into the sunshine.

"I will never see her again," Hi'iaka promised as tears flowed down her cheeks. "She was my sister, my guardian, one I loved above all others, but I will never see her again."

"Make no promises," Wahine-'ōma'o said. "Come, let us leave this place."

Wahine-'ōma'o led the way out of the tunnel and along the path to Ke-ala-ke-kua where they found Ka-lei-paoa's canoe. "Where is he?" Wahine-'ōma'o asked.

"He's gone to seek vengeance from Pele," came the answer.

"We will wait," Wahine-'ōma'o said. "He will not be long."

They waited four days. Hi'iaka sank deeply into sadness. She took no notice of the world around her. Wahine-'ōma'o forced her to eat, forced her to walk along the shore, massaged her, and tended her in all ways.

Even when Ka-lei-paoa came and said Pele had sent him to be Hi'iaka's husband, Hi'iaka did nothing more than meekly climb into the canoe. Not once did she look behind her as the island of Hawai'i with its immense mountains sank into the sea. She did not look back and see Pele staring out after the canoe. She never saw Pele again.

Hi'iaka would recover some of her old spirits, Wahine-'ōma'o vowed to herself. Someday she would accept that a live husband is better than a dead lover.

Wahine-'ōma'o shrugged her shoulders. The tale was not yet over. Wait and see, she told herself, wait and see. Then do what must be done. She saw twilight color the puffy clouds before her. Kaua'i was before them. After what had happened to them all, thought Wahine-'ōma'o, who could predict what was to come?

Nā Mele a Lohiʻau

CHRISTINE FAYÉ · 01

THE SONGS OF LOHI‘AU
Nā Mele a Lohi‘au

WIND FILLED THE SAILS and the small outrigger canoe sped across the ocean, water hissing at the bow, salt spray splashing Lohi‘au's face. Already O‘ahu was sinking into the sea and soon broad-topped Hā‘upu would appear before him. Greatly loved Hā‘upu, mountain whose shape announced, "Here is Kaua‘i of Kama-wae-lua-lani, here is home!"

Hi‘iaka was ahead of him, returning to Hā‘ena where she had brought him back to life. They had traveled together from Hā‘ena to Hale-ma‘uma‘u, she a dutiful messenger, he as husband to Pele. They had come to love one another, he and Hi‘iaka, although neither dared to say so for fear of the goddess. Only at the brink of Hale-ma‘uma‘u, after Hi‘iaka saw her ‘ōhi‘a lehua forests burned by Pele's fire, had Hi‘iaka embraced him. For that embrace he had died a second time, covered by the ashes and lava of Pele.

How long had he been a pillar of stone? He awoke to find himself in the presence of Kāne-milo-hai and Ka-moho-ali‘i, brothers of Pele, gods themselves. They had heard Hi‘iaka's cries of sorrow, they had stopped her from bringing the sea into the fire pit, they had heard her vow never to see Pele again, and had sadly watched her sail away from Hawai‘i forever. They had looked on all that remained of the man she loved, the man who had died twice because Pele could not contain her emotions, neither love nor anger. It was not the man's fault. If he had died twice, could he not be brought to life twice? So they combined their strength and broke apart the column of lava and recreated the man.

"Go," they told Lohi‘au, "sail to Kaua‘i. Hi‘iaka is there. Go to her." They had given him a canoe and now Hā‘upu was in sight and he would soon be home.

He caught a large swell and sped into the bay of Hana-mā‘ulu, between Ahu-kini and Pali-‘o‘o-ma. He beached the canoe near a fisherman's shed where two old men were sitting under a tree. They were polishing three māmaka, carrying sticks formed from branches of a kou tree. Two of the poles were v-shaped at the top to hold a crossbar when they were stuck into the ground. The crossbar itself had faces carved at each end. Beside them was a lidded gourd calabash in net wrapping.

"Welina ‘oe, welcome!" called one old man. "I am Ka-ua-le‘a."

"I am Ka-ua-noho," said the other old man. "Come and eat. You look as though you have traveled far."

"Indeed," answered Lohi'au. "To the land of Milu and back."

The old men brought out a calabash of poi, a handful of 'inamona to add flavor, a small bowl of hīnālea relish, some sweet potatoes and a piece of haupia and invited their guest to eat. They insisted on serving him. Ka-ua-noho even went to fetch his hand-held kahili and waved it gently over Lohi'au's food to keep the flies away. Ka-ua-le'a opened a coconut and offered their guest a drink. When his stomach was full, Lohi'au looked about him curiously.

"What are you doing with those māmake carrying sticks?" he asked.

"Ah, that is part of our present," Ka-ua-le'a said.

"We are giving a gift of a tapa bed sheet our wives have made," added Ka-ua-noho.

"Who is the lucky one?" asked Lohi'au.

"Hi'iaka-i-ka-poli-o-Pele," Ka-ua-le'a said. "But I am told she will not answer to that name. It is only Hi'iaka, she says."

"She is going to marry Ka-lei-paoa," Ka-ua-noho said.

"At Wai-pouli."

"Tomorrow."

"I would like to be there," said Lohi'au. Even as he listened to them, he was not surprised. It was logical that his friend Ka-lei-paoa would marry Hi'iaka to care for her. He ached to see them both again. Would they welcome him? Would they fear him?

"Come with us," the old men said as one.

"I have no gift for them," he said, shaking his head.

"Our present will be enough for the three of us," Ka-ua-noho said.

Ka-ua-le'a stuck one of the v-shaped poles into the ground and Ka-ua-noho placed the other. Between the two they laid crossbar and over that laid the piece of tapa bedding they took from the covered calabash. The top sheet was covered with intricate designs, as brightly colored as the mountain birds, so big that both ends almost touched the ground when laid over the crossbar. Lohi'au looked at this and nodded as an idea came to him.

"A surprise," he whispered to himself. "Let my coming be a surprise."

The old men offered him a place to sleep and when the first gleam of light touched the eastern horizon they woke him. Ka-ua-le'a slung the māmaka onto his shoulder and Ka-ua-noho carried the large calabash containing the tapa. They refused Lohi'au's offer to help and the three began walking along the beach toward Wai-lua. They found the place between the soft sand and the dappling waves where the sand is firm underfoot and chatted as they walked. The journey was pleasant and Lohi'au asked many questions of the coming wedding festivities. He nodded when they told him of the kilu game planned that very night. Kilu was a game of skill. One player tossed his oval of coconut shell ten times across a mat and had to strike the marker of his opposite in order to win. The game was always woman against man and the loser forfeited anything from a piece of land to an embrace. Before each toss, the contestant had to chant a song. Chant poorly, miss the toss, and the loser retired with much teasing. It was a game for the young.

"You both must enter the kilu contest," Lohi'au said.

"No, no," laughed Ka-ua-le'a. "I am too old for such goings on. I am no chanter."

"All you have to do is enter. I will do the chanting," Lohi'au said.

"I do not know how to chant either," Ka-ua-noho admitted. "How ashamed we will be if someone actually aims for our marker."

"And if you chant," said Ka-ua-le'a, "what fools we will look, a chant flowing from our closed mouths."

Lohi'au insisted. "There will be only two chants and I will teach them to you as we walk along. You will only have to mouth the words."

The elderly men were doubtful. People would laugh at them for there comes a time when the ti plant sags over the pali and a man has no business joining a kilu game.

"Besides," Ka-ua-le'a said, "Hi'iaka is the guest of honor. She will be the first to throw her kilu."

"Most likely at Ka-lei-paoa's marker," Ka-ua-noho said.

"She will laugh at us."

"No, you both must enter." Lohi'au commanded, a chief used to being obeyed. "I have a plan to surprise Hi'iaka and Paoa." Then he would say no more except, "You will see when the time comes."

Neither man had asked Lohi'au his name but they had recognized him since the story of his death had flown around the island in greater and greater detail. They knew his rank was greater than theirs. If he ordered them to enter the game, they would enter. Especially if he would do the hard part, the actual chanting. It was a trick of some sort, they thought, and grinned at the thought of being a part of it. They listened carefully as he sang the two chants he wanted them to learn.

Soon they stood on the banks of the Wai-lua where it flowed across its sandbar out to sea. Lohi'au looked for a canoe to take them across but the river was empty. "We must swim," he said.

"No, my lord," said Ka-ua-noho. "We are your canoe; we shall take you across."

Ka-ua-le'a extended his left hand and grasped his left elbow with his right hand. Ka-ua-noho did the same and the two took hold of each other's wrists and formed a chair.

"Sit, my lord," Ka-ua-le'a said. Putting his hands across their shoulders, Lohi'au sat and the men carried him across the sandbar where the swirling river threatened to carry them out to sea. When he was safely across, they returned for their bed sheet and māmaka.

They arrived at Wai-pouli as the sun sank behind Nounou hill and entered the compound where festivities had already begun. There was the booming of hula drums and the shrill piping of the nose flute, the rattle of the 'umeke and the hollow booms of the bamboo tubes. Children ran about underfoot, yelling and making noise as only children can. Men yelled, women chatted, there were snatches of song, and much laughter. Dogs yipped, pigs grunted, roosters crowed, hens clucked. The moon, so eager it had risen while the sun was still in the sky, shone down to add its luster to the flaming torches and the bonfires.

No one noticed when two elderly men entered the enclosure where the kilu game would be played. They came to the edge of the mat where the players sit and, at Lohi'au's instruction, placed their poles and laid the crossbar between them. The bed sheet brushed the ground and Lohi'au, parting the sides, entered into the tent it formed and sat down. No one could tell that there was a man hiding there. Ka-ua-le'a and Ka-ua-noho sat in front of the bed sheet and waited.

In time the lā anoano, the presiding referee of the game, entered the enclosure. He looked doubtfully at the two men. "What are you doing here?" he asked.

"We are waiting to play kilu," Ka-ua-le'a replied.

"You?" the lā anoano said, astonished. "Both of you?"

The two oldsters nodded.

The lā anoano laughed. "Why not?" he said. "I shall choose opponents fit for you."

People began to crowd into the kilu enclosure. Lohi'au longed to see what was happening, to catch a glimpse of Hi'iaka but he dared not move. No, the surprise must be complete.

The lā anoano arranged the players. On one side he placed Ka-lei-paoa, to the right of him he placed two young chiefs, and on the left he put the two old men. There was a buzzing of voices as the people saw this strange sight. "What is the lā anoano thinking of?" "It's shameful, two old men." "Old men are still men, let them play." "Hush!"

On the opposite side, facing the men, the lā anoano placed five women. Hi'iaka, with Wahine-'ōma'o at her shoulder, sat in the middle. Her head and shoulders drooped and she took no interest in anything about her. Two aliʻi wahine, chiefesses of the highest rank, were on either side of her.

The luna hoʻomalu stood up. He called out in a loud voice, "Pūheoheo, ea!"

Everyone cried out, "Pūheoheo, ea!" The game was under way. The people became very quiet. If anyone talked during the game, their clothes would be torn off and burned and they would have to slink home naked.

The lā anoano handed Hiʻiaka an ipu, a coconut shell slider that had been cut into an elliptical shape. She would slide it across the mat aiming to strike a wooden marker that stood in front of each man.

Wahine-ʻōmaʻo poked Hiʻiaka in the back, reminding her that this game was being conducted in her honor.

Hiʻiaka sighed, for Lohiʻau and she had played once long ago on Oʻahu, and now she did not care to play.

Wahine-ʻōmaʻo dug her sharply in the ribs again and motioning with her hand urged Hiʻiaka to stand and begin the game.

Hiʻiaka stood and looked at the men arrayed across the mat from her. Ka-lei-paoa, of course, was expected. The young men were as expected, too, and of no consequence. Then she saw the two old men with their markers in front of their knees, with big grins on their faces, for they knew she would not choose to throw against them.

Hiʻiaka indicated that she was ready to throw.

"Here is the beloved one, a kilu kiss," the luna hoʻomalu intoned. Hiʻiaka threw her slider with a flick of the wrist. It slid across the mat and squarely struck the marker in front of Ka-ua-noho.

"The beloved one is named," intoned the luna hoʻomalu. "What must he do?"

"Chant," said Hiʻiaka and sat down. For a moment she had enjoyed the look of surprise on Ka-lei-paoa's face. He had not expected that.

Ka-ua-noho placed his hands on his knees and opened his mouth. The audience was surprised at the youthful quality of his voice as it rose and fell in the studied cadence of the chant.

> "The saw-toothed hala leaves of Naue
> Quickly scratches and bruises the skin.
> We are pelted by firebrand embers
> Thrown from the cliffs of Ka-maile

Borne by the Lani-ku'u-wa'a wind.
The round firebrand scar of Kū-pono-aloha
Tells of the fire burning there,
The soaring fire of Ka-maile."

Hi'iaka half rose to her feet, then sank down again. She and Lohi'au had created that chant themselves to pass the time as they traveled to Hawai'i. How could this old man know her chant? It was impossible, yet he had sung it. Perhaps someone had overheard her and had repeated it and somehow this man had learned it. Thoughts buzzed through her like flies over an open calabash of poi.

Then the lā anoano handed back her ipu slider and the luna ho'omalu intoned, "Pūheoheo, ea!" and the audience repeated, "Pūheoheo, ea!"

Hi'iaka stood. "Here is the beloved one, a kilu kiss," the luna ho'omalu intoned. Hi'iaka threw her ipu with a flick of the wrist. It slid across the mat and squarely struck the marker in front of Ka-ua-le'a.

"The beloved one is named," intoned the luna ho'omalu. "What must he do?"

"Chant," said Hi'iaka and sat down.

Ka-ua-le'a cleared his throat. Then he opened his mouth and the sound of the chant filled the enclosure.

"Farewell, my companion of the misty rain
That sprinkled the lehua trees as we rested at noon
And wove wreaths in the rain that gives flowers life.
My lehua forest has been burned to embers,
Gone are those I love, Hōpoe and Lohi'au.
You are a warrior of wind against Pele-honua-mea.
I brought you to your death here at Pu'u-lena.
Your fate is the long sleep, death.
Farewell, Lohi'au, my love from Hā'ena.
Lohi'au, my love is yours."

This time there was no doubt. No one in the world could know this chant except one other. Hi'iaka once again felt the hot ashes falling on her, once again heard herself chanting this farewell into his ear as Lohi'au died.

Only one man could know that chant!

Hi'iaka ran across the mat and pulled on the sheet of tapa. Lohi'au sprang to his feet and with a cry of gladness, Hi'iaka wrapped her arms around him. He was warm, he was alive, he was hers, he was Lohi'au-ipo-o-Hā'ena and the next time he died they would go together.

Wahine-'ōma'o hugged herself in sheer happiness. Tears fell down her cheeks. She was not so happy that she did not notice the look of deep shame on Ka-lei-paoa's face or the look of despair as he left the assembly and plunged into the night.

There are those that say that Ka-lei-paoa fled into the sea because he was ashamed. He had sworn to avenge his friend's death and instead had become the lover of the deadly goddess. Ka-lei-paoa, they say, swam strongly along the path of moonlight until he came ashore on the floating island of Kū-ahi-lani and was never seen again.

Others say that Wahine-'ōma'o followed Ka-lei-paoa and met him on the beach and held him there. They say she reminded him that both she and he were companions of their chiefs and that their tour of duty was not yet over. Moreover, these people say, when Hi'iaka and Lohi'au returned to Hā'ena, Wahine-'ōma'o and Ka-lei-paoa were with them and that all four remained together for the rest of their days.

Wai-ʻauʻau-a-Hiʻiaka

CHRISTINE FAYE©99

BATHING POOL OF HIʻIAKA
Wai-ʻauʻau-a-Hiʻiaka

PELE-HONUA-MEA GROWS RESTLESS from time to time. Lying on her bed of lava, sleepless, sighing, turning from side to side, she feels the ache, loneliness caused by the absence of her sister, Hiʻiaka-i-ka-poli-o-Pele. She had carried Hiʻiaka in her bosom, had sent her on the errand to Kauaʻi to return with Lohiʻau. Impatient, her swiftly rising anger overpowering her, Pele accused her sister of wrong-doing and covered Lohiʻau with hot ash. Hiʻiaka had left, swearing never again to look upon the face of her sister. Pele, in the long silent nights remembers and weeps. From time to time a desire to see her sister once again causes Pele to send out her spiritual form to Kauaʻi where Hiʻiaka lives.

On this late afternoon, Pele stood on the plains of Kīpū at the foot of Hāʻupu mountain where her enemy Kamapuaʻa sometimes returns in his cloud form to bring rain.

Here, long ago, Pele and Kamapuaʻa, the black hog man, had met. Pele had been saved only by the timely coming of her sister Kapo-ʻula-kinaʻu. She had lured Kamapuaʻa away with her very special charms. Pele rose from the ground and began to climb toward the gap leading to Kīpū-kai. A breeze descending from Hāʻupu brought the refreshing perfume of mokihana with it. Pele stopped to look over the Puna plain, the Hulā-ʻia river cutting deeply into the plain just below her, the gentle swell of Kilohana, a volcanic cinder of great symmetry where no fire had risen when she struck deep into the earth with Paoa, her stick of power, the ridge from Kālepa to Mauna-kapu and on to the sharp peaks of Kalalea and Ka-hoku-ʻalele that marked the end of Puna and the beginning of Koʻolau.

Beside her, Hiʻiaka took on her human form. She stretched and glanced at her dirt-streaked and aged sister. "Pele," Hiʻiaka whispered. "I need to bathe and so do you. I need to drink my fill of fresh water."

Pele looked about her. "There is no water near by," she said. "And I am tired."

"Strike with your sacred staff," answered Hiʻiaka. "Cause water to come forth."

"Paoa's strike should bring forth fire, not water!" Pele said angrily but as quickly as it rose, her anger subsided, and she sighed deeply. She struck the earth lightly with the sacred staff. A gentle flow of water bubbled to the surface and trickled down, forming a little pool before flowing down to join the waters of the Hulā-ʻia stream. The two sisters bathed and refreshed themselves and remained there that night listening to the spring's song.

This spring of Pele was afterwards called Wai-'au'au-a-Hi'iaka, the fresh bathing water of Hi'iaka.

So on this late afternoon Pele rested beside Hā'upu on the road to Kīpū-kai. Her heart filled with longing for her sister and she remembered the spring where they had bathed so long ago. Pele went to the spring she had made for her sister, went to Wai-'au'au-a-Hi'iaka, but when she got there, the spring no longer flowed. There was only a dry rock basin.

"Auwē," said Pele in puzzlement. "The spring should be here."

A ripple of laughter filled Pele's ears. She turned angrily. Further up the hillside she saw two young women on either side of a pool of fresh water. One sat beneath a kukui tree whose long, slender leaves resembled the rush grass that grew on sandy beaches. The other leaned against a kukui tree whose leaves gave off a sour smell in the gentle breeze of evening.

Pele strode up the hill to the pond and demanded, "What spring feeds this pool?"

"It is called Wai-'au'au-a-Hi'iaka," one young woman answered

"Not so," answered Pele. "I know where that spring should be. I created it down there. Who dared to move my spring?"

"Moved it is, indeed," answered the woman leaning against the sour-leafed kukui tree. "Our husband moved it for us to give us a better view."

"Who then are you?" asked Pele. "And who is your husband who dares to move my spring?"

"I am Kukui-lau-mānienie," answered she whose leaves resembled the seashore grass.

"And I am Kukui-lau-hanahana," answered the other, still leaning against her sour-leafed tree.

"And our husband is Kamapua'a, whom you know well, O Pele!" said Kukui-lau-mānienie.

"Kamapua'a?" she muttered. "Even now he comes to mock me." She glared at the two women. "How dare you bathe in my spring?" Pele demanded.

"Where indeed is your spring?" laughed Kukui-lau-hanahana. "You found no home on Kaua'i. You own no spring of water here."

"I planted a clean spring there on that rock below," said Pele. "I made it as a bathing place for my sister."

"You have no water here," Kukui-lau-mānienie insisted. "This spring was given to us and moved here for our pleasure by Kamapua'a before he left us to sail for Kahiki. Here we shall wait for his return."

"Kamapua'a was wrong to do that," cried Pele, anger flashing from her eyes like bolts of lightning. "I shall return this spring to its proper place."

"You cannot do that," answered the women. "Kamapua'a warned us that you would come, Pele, goddess of fire, red-eyed and old. "

"Be careful," muttered Pele. "My anger grows. I shall destroy you."

"Pele, Pele, great firemaker," taunted the women. "Listen to the words our husband Kamapua'a told us. You would come, he told us, in your spirit form. Tell Pele, he said, tell Pele she cannot move her spring again. Great is the power of Kamapua'a. Greater than the power of Pele, the red-eyed eater of bird food!"

Pele gestured toward the maidens as if to kill them with her magic powers. The two young women laughed and splashed water on her. "Pele, do you forget?" they laughed. "Your body lies sleeping at Kī-lau-ea, your sacred staff Paoa beside you there in the cold. You do not have the power to hurt us now!"

Bitterness filled her heart at the mocking taunts of the maidens, taunts that Kamapua'a had taught them. Pele looked more closely at the two sisters. Behind their fair faces and long hair, behind their bodies as they sat leaning on their trees, she saw the outlines of something quite different. Pele laughed. "No, I cannot hurt you and you are right, in my spirit form I do not have the strength to move the spring of water. But no matter, for I see Kamapua'a has already revenged himself on you."

The eyes of Kukui-lau-hanahana and Kukui-lau-mānienie filled with tears and they began to wail in grief. "You are right, Pele," Kukui-lau-hanahana said. "He taught us a bitter lesson."

"We must remain here until Kamapua'a returns," added Kukui-lau-mānienie.

"That will be a long time away," Pele said. "Endless, indeed, is your wait. Guard my spring well."

"We will," the sisters promised. As they spoke, their bodies and the trees they leaned against faded away and only two large rocks remained, all that remained of their earthly forms.

Be careful now, when you bathe in the spring water of Wai-'au'au-a-Hi'iaka in the shadow of Hā'upu. The guardians of the spring are still there, one on each side of the pond. Be careful!

AFTERWORD

FOURTEEN GENERATIONS BEFORE THE ARRIVAL OF CAPTAIN COOK, the ali'i nui, ruling chief, of Kaua'i was Kūkona. During his reign he succeeded in uniting the entire island into one kingdom. The final battle between Puna and Kona is told in this book. He also defeated the invading army of Ka-lau-nui-o-Hua of Hawai'i island and could have become the first ali'i nui of all the islands. Instead he chose to impose a promise that no chief would ever again invade Kaua'i. This peace lasted over six hundred years. These are significant events in the history of this island.

In addition, during Kūkona's life, there came extraordinary visitors from the south to join their lives with the inhabitants of Kaua'i. These people had great adventures here and their larger-than-life personalities helped ancient chanters to create epic poems about them. Lesser storytellers found many humorous and moral anecdotes ideal for telling to an enthralled audience by the smokey light of kukui oil lamps.

The first visitor was Kapo-'ula-kina'u. A story, "Hanakā'ape" in *More Kaua'i Tales*, tells of the first time Kapo-'ula-kina'u possessed another person. Her legacy of the medical practices for mental diseases made Kaua'i famous in certain circles. After she left Kaua'i, she eventually settled on Moloka'i. There she became a goddess of sorcery, much prayed to by priests intent on praying a victim to death. Her deep knowledge of hula, however, helped her become a patron goddess of the hula at the famous school at Kē'ē, Hā'ena.

Her daughter Kapo-ino-kai became the ancestress of Kaua'i ruling chiefs after her time, beginning with her son Kaumaka-a-Manō, a noted hunter of the great white shark.

Another visitor, Kapo-'ula-kina'u's sister, was Pele-honua-mea. She left Kaua'i to find a dry home where she would be safe from her vengeful sister Nā-maka-o-Kaha'i, goddess of the ocean. Very quickly, Pele became the goddess of the volcano at Hale-ma'uma'u at Kī-lau-ea, Hawai'i. She lives there still surrounded by members of her family, the Hi'iaka sisters, her shark brother Ka-moho-ali'i and others. She leads a restless life, even today, and she can still be seen from time to time on Kaua'i in the form of either an elderly woman or a young beauty. "Weoweo-pilau," in *More Kaua'i Tales*, tells of one such visit of Pele to Kaua'i.

Hi'iaka-i-ka-poli-o-Pele and Lohi'au presumably lived the rest of their natural human lives at Kē'ē, Hā'ena. Certainly the hālau hula at the end of the road remains a sacred place that holds their memory. Pāʻū-o-palaʻe's name was given to the lower wet cave there, and Hiʻiaka's uncle's name, Ka-moho-aliʻi, was given the cliff above the cave. The housesite of Lohiʻau is still visible and his sister's name is given to the sand dunes to the west of Lima-huli stream, Ka-hua-nui.

Kamapuaʻa, part pig, part man, became a demi-god and he, too, like Pele, can be seen from time to time in various places on the island. Transporting raw pork without the proper prayers and offerings, it is said, can be dangerous.

Lima-loa, brother of Lohiʻau, lived on for centuries in the famous mirage of Mānā. How he came to enter the mirage is told in "Ka Liʻulā o Mānā" in *Polihale*. He could be seen there on certain nights of the moon, until the swamp and lakes were drained to make room for sugar cane. Then the mirage disappeared forever, taking Lima-loa and his love, Lāʻie-i-ka-wai, with it.

Sources

Those wishing to read the original sources for my stories in this book may look in the following:

Akina, J.A. *He Moolelo no ka Poe Menehune*. Unpublished manuscript. 1905.

Anderson, J.C. *Myths and Legends of the Polynesians*. Rutland: Charles E. Tuttle Co. 1974.

Andrews, L. *A Dictionary of the Hawaiian Language*. Rutland: Charles E. Tuttle Co. 1974.

Beckwith, M. *Hawaiian Mythology*. Honolulu: University of Hawai'i Press. 1970.

Emerson, N.B. *Pele and Hiiaka*. Rutland: Charles E. Tuttle Co. 1980.

—. *Unwritten Literature of Hawaii*. Rutland: Charles E. Tuttle Co. 1980.

Fornander, W.C. *An Account of the Polynesian Race, Its Origins and Migrations and the Ancient History of the Hawaiian People to the Times of Kamehameha I*. Rutland: Charles E. Tuttle Co. 1969.

—. *Fornander Collection of Hawaiian Antiquities and Folk-Lore*. Bishop Mus. Memoirs, vols 4-6. Honolulu: Bishop Museum Press, 1816-20.

Kalakaua, D. *The Legends and Myths of Hawaii*. Rutland, VT: Charles E. Tuttle Co., 1972.

Knudsen, E.K. *Teller of Tales, Tall Stories from Old Kauai*. Honolulu: Mutual Publishing, 1946.

Malo, D. *Hawaiian Antiquities*. Rev. ed. Translated by N.B. Emerson. B.P. Bishop Mus. Spec. Pub. 2. Honolulu: Bishop Museum Press, 1951.

Pukui, M.K. and S.H. Elbert. *Hawaiian Dictionary*. Honolulu: University of Hawai'i Press, 1986.

Rice, W.H. *Hawaiian Legends*. B.P. Bishop Mus. Bull. 3. Millwood, NY: Kraus Reprint Co., 1971.

Thrum, T.G., compiler. *Hawaiian Folk Tales*. Chicago: A.D. McClurg & Co., 1907.

—. *More Hawaiian Folk Tales*. Chicago: A.D. McClurg & Co., 1923.

Westervelt, W.D. Hawaiian Historical Legends. Rutland, Vt: Charles E. Tuttle Co., 1972.

—. *Myths and Legend of Hawaii*. Honolulu: Mutual Publishing, 1987.

Wichman, Frederick B. *Kaua'i Tales*. Honolulu: Bamboo Ridge Press, 1985.

—. *Polihale and other Kaua'i Legends*. Honolulu: Bamboo Ridge Press, 1991.

—. *More Kaua'i Tales*. Honolulu: Bamboo Ridge Press, 1997.

—. *Kaua'i: Ancient Place-Names and Their Stories*. Honolulu: University of Hawai'i Press, 1998.

About the Author

Frederick B. Wichman has written three other collections of legends from the island of Kauaʻi: *Kauaʻi Tales, Polihale and Other Kauaʻi Legends,* and *More Kauaʻi Tales.* He is also the author of *Kauaʻi, Ancient Place Names and Their Stories.* His tales have been turned into plays and hulas, narrated by professional storytellers, used in university classes, and even used as sources for quilt patterns. He has been designated a "Living Treasure of Kauaʻi" by the Kauaʻi Museum.

About the Illustrator

Christine Fayé grew up on sugar plantations all over Hawaiʻi. Since 1980 she has operated a small business on Kauaʻi as a full-time artist specializing in graphic design, illustration, and interpretive exhibits. She received the 1993 Ka Palapala Poʻokela Excellence in Illustration Award from the Hawaiʻi Book Publishers Association for her pointillism-style of pen and ink illustrations for *Kauaʻi Tales.* Two of the drawings in *Pele Mā* received State Foundation on Culture and the Arts Acquisition Awards.